The Pirate's Curse

A Perry Normal Adventure Book 6

Mason Stone

Dedicated to all those who love pirate stories.

To Pig, who keeps my heart in her treasure chest.

Disclaimer

This is a work of fiction, and the depiction of persons, places and circumstances is fictional. This material, however, is based on both anecdotal and factual records and accounts. Any relationship to real persons or organizations is purely coincidental.

ISBN 978-1-989386-04-0

CONTENTS

PART I   THE MISTS OF TIME

CHAPTER ONE   RETURN TO SUNNY FLORIDA

"Perry! You'd better have a *good* reason to call me at 5 a.m.!"

"Wake up, Henry," said Perry, "it's an e-mail from Capt. Thom Dean in Ft. Lauderdale. He wants us to join him on a treasure hunt for the lost galleon Concepción lost off Hispaniola in 1641. "

"The Spanish galleon? Bringing tons of gold, silver and emeralds back to Spain? Does he know where it is?"

Henry was wide awake now!

"He says he has maps that indicate where it foundered in a storm.

Strange thing is, it was already plundered in 1687 by an English adventurer named William Phips and much of the treasure was recovered and given to King James II of England!"

"So why would Capt. Dean go looking now-- over 300 years later?"

"That's exactly what I intend to find out, Henry! Let's see if our parents will sponsor our little adventure like they did last time[Ψ].

Remember, all we have to do to persuade them that we will get something of value, like what my mom calls a 'growth experience'. Parents are always willing to help their children learn more about the world.

Let's meet at The Malt Shop later and we can consult with our trusty gang of friends!"

***

"You are going to go to Florida again? Didn't you nearly get yourself killed by some treasure-hunting maniac last time?" asked Charmaine.

"True," said Perry, "only it's a *different* maniac this time--who is not likely to wish Henry or me harm.

It's an old seaman who hangs around the harbor at Fort Lauderdale and is retired, from the service. Henry and I bumped into him when we were attending dive school to get our PADI license. He has cool stories about shipwrecks and the Bermuda Triangle and stuff."

[Ψ] See: *Perry Normal and the Mystery of Lost Atlantis*

" Why is he interested in going to sea with a couple of science geeks from Brackendale, New York?" said Robert-- with his characteristic tone of either irony or outright sarcasm.

"Perry found that tablet that came from Atlantis— don't you remember, Robert?" Max was getting into the fray now.

"Yeah, and he found gold coins just offshore using nothing but his eyes—and intelligent analysis of the seabed," said Margot.

Margot was bright—very bright—and like Henry was a whiz at Math. She was an Honor Student at Brackendale Middle School. She was also close to everyone in their gang and her opinion was respected.

"Capt. Dean says he needs some help to make this trip—he can skipper the boat while Henry and I dive on the wreck."

"If you can find it," said Robert, stuffing fries and gravy into his mouth.

"What *about* that, Perry?" said Rita. "There must be hundreds of shipwrecks off the Florida coast. How could you find *that particular ship*?"

"We are counting on Capt. Dean's long experience at sea, and with maps. His hobby was studying nautical maps and lore," said Perry confidently.

"Study is one thing, Perry, but navigating those treacherous waters looking for something that has been submerged for centuries is another!" Charmaine warned.

Charmaine was like the official den mother of the eight or so kids who made up The Malt Shop Gang. She was going into Eighth Grade—like all of them—but was way more mature than her years. Besides, she was fun.

"What do your parents say?" Charmaine continued.

"We have a preliminary presentation to make tonight to both sets of parents," said Henry. "With any luck, our summer holiday—which starts in, what, eleven days—is going to be a doozy! Anyone want to join us?"

"Naw, got summer school," Max said dolefully. "I failed Math. Just by, like, ten lousy marks! Anyhow, there's goes July."

"I've gotta work," said Charmaine.

"I'm volunteering—along with Rita—at the senior's home. Need I remind you all that you have to accumulate 100 hours of certified volunteer experience before you can graduate high school," said Margot. "Better get started, people!"

"Let us know if your parents approve, and good luck, you guys!" said Rita and Max.

"You'll be the first to know," said Henry confidently.

***

"Have we met him?" said Lisa Normal—Perry's mom--right as soon as they started the conversation.

"I told you about him, I think," said Perry, looking doubtful. "We passed him every day by the pier at Lauderdale. He used to be a ship's captain! In the Navy!"

"And why would you trust him to do what he is proposing—take you two characters out on the open sea, supposedly looking for Spanish treasure?"

Now it was Henry's mom Sherry asking the questions.

"Well, Mrs. Schuyler, sometimes you have to go with your gut, and my gut tells me this guy is legit," said Perry looking her right in the eye.

Later Henry asked him: "Where did you get that line? 'Legit'?? You sound like a mobster!"

"Hah, Henry! I heard it on The Simpsons."

"Oh my gawd—well, it worked! My parents are going to pay all my expenses, provided I give them Capt. Dean's credentials and they get a letter of intent signed by him."

"My parents will consent provided that we meet up with them in August at the Embassy Hotel—same one we stayed in last time, remember?"

"Yeah, they had excellent room service!" said Henry, bringing the conversation around to food, as he often did.

"We leave in nine days. Better get things organized, my old friend," said Perry.

Indeed, they had been friends for many years and expected to be for many years to come.

***

Sunny Florida is a paradise in the summer. The beaches, and the warmth that the Great Lakes region rarely gets, and if it does—it comes with the humidity that comes all the way up from the Gulf of Mexico.

Thousands of visitors from everywhere crowd the clean white sands that go all the way down to the Florida Keys, close to Cuba.

Capt. Dean met the boys with a hearty handshake.

"I wasn't sure you would be able to come, or even be willing to trust the old Captain," said Thom Dean, a man of about 61, widowed and pensioned, and resident of Fort Lauderdale for some years now.

He led them to a local diner where seafood brunch was always on the menu. The boys—like *all* boys—were starving. That's probably why America is the home of 'all you can eat' buffets!

"So let me outline the plan for you, Perry and Henry," the old salt began.

"Not only do I have current nautical maps of the waters around the north side of Hispaniola—you know your geography? Dominican Republic and Haiti nowadays—but I have a journal that I found in an old bookstore in Miami that gives *more*, not just the common lore about the wreck site."

Perry put down his fork; Henry just kept shoveling shrimp into his mouth.

"There is more treasure than Phips or anyone else has brought to the surface.

A gold statue of the Madonna that was made by native artisans in Peru. Worth a fortune!

People assumed it went down with a fleet of ships in the hurricane of 1705 near Havana. But my source has a more detailed and accurate inventory of what was aboard the *Concepción* when she met her fate.

That is why I have chartered a larger boat—75 feet—with a power winch and steel cable baskets for hauling heavier items up from the depths of the sea.

Is this getting more interesting for you, boys?"

Now Henry put his fork down too.

"And what makes you so sure—even if we find the wreck—that we can legally salvage the treasure?" he said.

Henry had learned from their search for lost Atlantis that there are federal and state laws regarding recovery and salvage of wrecks in U.S. waters.

"What is the key to our getting rich," Capt. Dean chuckled, "is that this is in international waters where the 'finders, keepers' rule applies. There are no laws on the high seas, a fact that allowed buccaneers to plunder at will."

"Oh man! What I would give to go back to the Golden Age of Pirates," said Henry.

"Well, we have modern equipment and methods of navigation those pirates could only dream of!" said Capt. Dean.

"So if we are successful and find treasure, it's *ours to keep?* said Perry.

"That's right, boys! From the smallest doubloon to the 150-pound ingots of silver and gold that have been found on such Spanish shipwrecks.

We could *all* retire!" Capt. Dean was stuffing his pipe and striking a match to light it. Puffs of fragrant blue smoke rose in the air on the patio where they were sitting.

The pleasant heat of the sun made the boys sleepy.

"We are staying at the Embassy," said Perry. "Give us an idea of when we ship out, Capt. Dean."

"I have a few preparations left to make. Day after tomorrow—at dawn—is what I'm thinking."

"At which pier is the ship moored? What's her name?"

"Pier 13. She's a twin-engine diesel with flying bridge and she is called the *Mary Celeste*."

"Wait a minute..." Henry started to say, but Perry quickly covered Henry's mouth with his hand.

"Great!" said Perry. "We'll see you then!"

"Why'd you cover my mouth, Perry? We both know the legend of the real *Marie Celeste* that was found abandoned near the Azores with no one aboard! Man, it is not a lucky name for a ship!"

"I just didn't want you to blurt that out in front of the captain, that's all. He's invested a lot of money and time to get this expedition off the ground.

Any private misgivings we may have should be kept between *us*, Henry.

Let's just go with the flow and see where it takes us."

The boys brushed their teeth and turned out the lights. In just over 24 hours, they would be setting sail on an adventure never to be forgotten!

CHAPTER TWO   THE SPANISH MAIN

"Mariners are a superstitious lot," Capt. Dean was saying as the big diesels throbbed and the *Mary Celeste* left a wake of bubbles and foam behind it.

"Everything from not having a cat or a corpse on board, to the notion that some ships are just plain unlucky—or are cursed."

Both boys felt a sudden chill and grabbed their windbreakers; but it was not the breeze, it was the thought of curses and unnatural phenomena that every sailor dreaded.

Even in the modern age of psychology and brain research, we can only speculate about the mental and emotional stresses sailors over the centuries have endured.

Did they hallucinate sea monsters? Most folklore about the sea mentions them. Perhaps it was deprivation of food and water that drove men mad at sea.

Perry and Henry were curious, but not much interested in having first-hand experience.

"Some stories say that if you find treasure on a cursed ship, and you bring it to the surface—you will never return to port."

"There are many hazards at sea, Captain, which would better explain why men fail to return," said Perry.

"You are not going to tell us that the *Concepción* is said to be a cursed ship, are you Captain?" said Henry with some concern.

"Not that I know of," said the captain. "Why would I risk everything just for a few million dollars?"

The boys weren't sure if he were being facetious or not.

"Have we got radio so we can relay a distress signal—I mean—if we had to?" said Henry.

"We have all the latest hi-tech gear, boys. GPS, radar, shortwave radio—the works! This baby's got more toppings than a deluxe pizza!"

The captain shouldn't have mentioned 'pizza'! Poor Henry was now craving pizza more than anything in this world. He had to stand at the rail and grip it tight for a few moments. It might be a long time till he had a good slice of pepperoni with mushrooms and olives, green peppers, and...

"You okay, Henry?" Perry butted into his reverie.

"Yeah, just a little hungry. You know how the sea air affects your appetite."

"Sure. We'll rustle up some grub—as the captain likes to say—in an hour or so. Hang in there, Henry!" Perry tried to sound encouraging.

At that moment—as if to verify Captain Dean's faith in technology, the marine radio snapped to life as an announcement came over the frequency band:

This is a bulletin to mariners, particularly to small craft. The Coast Guard has received intelligence that tropical storm Ivan is showing extreme activity as it enters the Caribbean region. All ships are to be alert and ready to put into port. This is a Code Yellow alert. I repeat—Code Yellow.

The raspy metallic voice ceased and the sound of swells slapping against the hull were again the dominant sound.

"When we see whitecaps, then we'll consider turning around," said Captain Dean.

"Let's grab some grub," he said—meaning 'eat breakfast'. The small propane stove burned hot, and soon scrambled eggs and bacon, toast and fries (pre-cooked) were on their plates and fast disappearing down their throats.

"I make real good coffee, fellas," the captain said. "I roast my own green beans and grind 'em and use the best of what Costa Rica and Colombia can offer us."

"We don't drink coffee as a rule," said Perry "but something hot to drink would be nice right now."

The wind had shifted and the sky was clouding over quite quickly, causing the temperature to drop a few degrees.

Other than a freighter steaming north--using the Gulf Stream to propel its progress--there seemed to be no other vessels of any kind out there.

Captain Dean appeared to be talking to his instruments.

"What the devil is going on?" he said to his compass in particular.

Without warning, a peculiar mist or fog suddenly enveloped their boat. It was hard to see the stern from the bow it was so thick. Perry was glad there were no other craft nearby since many collisions at sea occur during such times of fog and poor visibility.

"What's wrong with the compass, Captain?" said Perry, more to comfort Henry than the Captain.

"Damned if I know," said Capt. Dean. "It's spinning on its axis like I've never seen. Impossible!"

The moment he said 'spinning' the boat lurched sideways and started to rotate—slowly at first— counter-clockwise. Faster and faster it swung like a crazy merry-go-round, and all the crew could do was hold on to something.

Henry fell down and rolled under a lifeboat davit. Perry put a harness around his shoulders and sank to the deck. Captain Dean opened a mahogany chest full of lifejackets, yanked several of them out--piled in-- slamming the lid behind him. Before long, they had lost consciousness as the boat madly continued to whirl until it could no longer be seen in the mist.

***

"Morning," said Henry as he stood up on deck.

"Morning," said Perry rubbing his eyes.

"Morning? How is it morning?" said Capt. Dean looked wildly around their vessel which was bobbing in the sparkling sunlight of the bay.

"And where the hell are we?" he said, clearly astonished by the view he beheld. "Looks like the Virgin Islands if I am not mistaken. How did we get three hundred miles south of our prior position?"

The engines were off and cool to the touch. The compass reading showed they were bearing 160 degrees--which made it south-southeast--although the landscape was visibly Caribbean.

Several large sailing ships were on a course due west—meaning inbound to Cuba, Mexico, South America.

"There must be a regatta or tall ships festival, " said Captain Dean. "They haven't had ships like those in three hundred years. Boy, they are beauties!"

"You mean replicas of original European design?" said Henry.

"They have strangely dressed people on board," noticed Perry. "Costumes, I presume?"

"Ahoy!" came a booming voice from astern and they all turned at the same time to be looking at the bow of a sloop—easily identified by its sleek and low profile.

Its master was also dressed in period costume and the men of the *Mary Celeste* were convinced they had happened upon an event to celebrate Columbus' discovery of The New World, or maybe the Spanish conquest of just about everything in Central and South America, or--.

"Ahoy yourself," shouted Capt. Dean.

The men on the sloop were speaking English but with a peculiar accent that made them sound like they were reading Shakespeare. That's what Henry said.

"What manner of craft is it ye have there?" said the master—a handsome fellow with skin as brown as a bowrail.

Ye've lost yer sails, have ye?"

Perry realized something was strange about this situation.

First of all, they never had sails—they were a motor powered vessel, like most.

"Where ye be headed, cap'n?" said the mate leaning far out over the gunwales along with the rest of a crew of about twelve. All were gawking at the funny boat with a flying bridge and no masts.

Captain Dean was in no mood to reveal their mission to find lost treasure. *I don't know these men from Adam*, he said in a low voice.

"Oh, just out for a cruise," he said lamely.

"A cruise is it?" Dean could see no one on the sloop believed a word of it.

"Ye've any cargo, cap'n?" said the master.

"No, nothing—just a cruise for the day."

"Ye must be mad, man!

Ye're in the middle of the Caribbean Sea with a ship with no sails, no crew to speak of, no cargo and no destination!

God be wit' ye, Cap'n."

And as suddenly as it had appeared, the graceful sailboat swung its boom to catch the rising breezes, and vanished to the west.

"That was weird," said Henry.

"Totally," said Perry.

"Capt. Dean? Ahh—maybe we should be making for land or some port or other. Maybe they're right and we are out in the open sea going...somewhere. Hispaniola? Where is that in relation to where we are now?" Henry was asking.

"I'm checking the GPS as we speak," he said.

"That can't be right! It says we are Latitude 18.3434 degrees North, longitude 64.8963 West. The closest port is Charlotte Amalie in the U.S. Virgin Islands.

"That puts us a hundred and ten nautical miles east of Hispaniola--and our treasure," the captain said.

Let's fire up the engines and set a course for the islands."

The roaring of the big engines was comforting. It signified the power to get out of whatever situation they were in.

Soon, the ship was churning toward a distant speck—and a safe haven!

***

The traffic in the sheltered port was mainly small boats with fishermen who looked with wonder and fear at their 75 foot monster with no sails and bubbles and thunder coming from the stern.

Capt. Dean cut the engines, and they dropped anchor about a hundred yards offshore.

He hailed another sailboat also resting at anchor.

"Ahoy! Is this the American Virgin Islands?"

"What is 'American' dear fellow," said the man standing in the bow.

He was flying the British colors on his masthead. His sailboat looked like something out of the 17th Century. Elegant but ancient.

"American. From America. The United States?"

"I have heard of an American colony in Virginia and there's some Englishmen in Massachusetts—is that how you say it? Are you gentlemen from there?"

Perry looked at Henry and Henry looked at Perry.

Then they both looked at Capt. Dean.

"In a way, I suppose. This may sound like a stupid question, but—what year is it?"

"Why it's 1691 old chap," said the Englishman.

"I am a junior officer in the Royal Navy of his Majesty King James II."

"*Six-teen-ninety-one*? Are you serious?"

Capt. Dean spoke for all of them.

"You chaps seemed to be like fish out of water. Why don't you come ashore and share a meal with my family. We own property here."

"Say 'yes', Captain Dean," whispered Henry.

"Why thank you, sir, ah..."

"Lord Brackendale, at your service." He extended a welcoming hand to Captain Dean and said: "Follow me!" and he trotted down the pier ahead of them.

"Did he say '*Brackendale*'?" Henry whispered into Perry's right ear.

"Brackendale," said Perry. "What are the odds?"

"We are like Alice in Wonderland here. Nothing is normal and everything is just plain weird!"

"Agreed," said Perry. "Let's see what Lady Brackendale serves for dinner, shall we?"

"Oh how love-ly George. You've brought guests and I've just roasted a lamb. How do you *do*?"

Lady Brackendale didn't look like she had been anywhere near a kitchen. She was elegantly dressed-- not what you'd expect in the tropics, and had a long string of pearls around her neck.

"Do sit down. I am Eleanor, and you are--?"

Captain Dean removed his cap and brushed his dirty fingers through his hair.

He introduced himself and the boys and tucked a white linen napkin under his collar--as if he had been an invited guest all along--at the Governor's mansion!

"I am the Governor of our little colony," explained Lord Brackendale, sipping a goblet of red wine.

"Matty? Serve our guests some wine, please. And bring some fresh bread."

The servant bowed and returned with the requested items.

"There is talk of a new government in England," said the governor. "I dearly hope that it won't affect my position here. Eleanor and I are quite comfortable. And if it weren't for those damned buccaneers and freebooters..."

His face flushed deeply for a moment and then he regained his composure.

"Matty? Our younger guests likely won't want the claret—squeeze some oranges and lemons into a cup and add some hot tea to it.

You do like tea?" said George.

"Sure, thank you, Lord Brackendale," said Perry.

"No need to be so formal in my house, boys. Call me George--my wife does."

It was hard to tell if he was making a little joke, but the tea was quite refreshing.

"Vitamin C," hissed Henry to Perry. Perry nodded.

"So what was your last port of call, Captain Dean?"

"Fort Lauderdale in Florida," he replied.

"Florida? You said 'Florida'? That's Spanish territory, isn't it?"

Lord Brackendale poured more wine for his wife and for Capt. Dean.

"Well, *this* part's *not*. It's a...*free* port, ah, has a lot of commercial traffic...from across the sea." Captain Dean was over a barrel.

"Oh, I see--*slaves*, you mean?"

"Well, if it makes a dol...*money,* you can find just about anything traded in and out of our harbor."

"Jolly good!" said George. "I've been writing endless letters to London but to no effect. Parliament is in disorder, and there's talk of a Protestant King planning to replace our present Catholic one. Why do they have to let religion ruin everything?" he said indignantly.

"Am I right, darling?" he said to his wife Eleanor.

"You are *always* right, George," she said, smiling.

On their way back to the *Mary Celeste*, the boys were complaining: "We could have slept in a real bed with real sheets! Why did you say we had to get back to the boat?"

Perry was clearly upset with Captain Dean's decision.

"I was suffocating in there!" said the captain. "I couldn't stand to hear them go on babbling in that stuffy upper-class English manner. That's why I don't watch that soap opera on PBS, what's it? Something 'Manor'."

The night was comfortably cool after the heat of the day, and the fragrance of some exotic flower drifted over the tiny harbor.

At length, Capt. Dean could be heard snoring like a diesel, and the boys fell into a deep sleep full of troubled dreams.

***

They left when the first peach blossom colors of dawn came into the east.

Keeping the engines at half-speed so they would run quiet, they soon found themselves at sea.

They were not alone. Massive brigantines and schooners plied these waters constantly. None seemed to pay much notice to the *Mary Celeste* and her crew.

"I'm glad you remembered to refill our water jugs at their well, Perry. I would have forgotten."

The captain was doing an inventory of their food and other supplies.

"Six days is what I estimate we have until our cupboards are completely bare." Captain Dean removed his cap and scratched his head.

"We have enough fuel to make one more port. You didn't see a fuel depot there by any chance, did you?"

"I'm going to say it, Captain, because we need to face the reality here," Perry said in a serious tone.

"I don't think we are in a quaint little cultural bubble here, and it's not 2018 anymore.

I think we time-slipped and it really is 1691.

Which means we are stranded.

We are not going to find a gas station for pleasure boats, we are not going to find a Seven-Eleven to get some sodas, and we are up shit creek without a paddle!"

Perry was upset to the point of being hysterical.

Henry was actually weeping.

Capt. Dean sat down with a heavy thud on the lifejacket chest he hid in during the storm.

"You're right. We have gone through a time portal to a different time, another world that existed long before there was an NFL franchise in Miami.

I don't have a clue what to do."

"Well if there's a pirate curse on treasure seekers, we didn't even get to the treasure!"

Perry was yelling and stomping all over the deck beside the galley hatchway. Even on a 75-foot boat, there is precious little deck space or any space in which to move if you are restless.

"Okay, let's head south to Martinique which has a bigger port I believe. It is French territory--even today. There may be a place where we can hole up and moor the boat until we figure out what to do."

Not having any better idea, the boys agreed and an hour and a half later the luscious green island with the steaming volcano hove into view.

"I don't like islands with volcanoes," Perry muttered. "I have bad memories."

"Santorini, right?" Henry remembered Perry's time travel episode to the ancient Greek island[v].

"Know any French, Henry? Or should I say *"Henri?"* Perry was in a better mood now that they were in port.

---

[v] *Perry Normal & The Riddle of the Time-slips*

They were immediately surrounded by curious fishermen in skiffs and small boats, men and boys bare-chested and barefoot.

"*Bonjour!*" tried Henry with as much enthusiasm as he could muster.

"We speak English," one man standing with his feet anchored on both gunwales of his boat. "We could hear you a mile away."

They meant Perry yelling.

"Welcome to our little island. *Bienvenue.*

You have perhaps something to trade with us?

We see you have metal ropes and tools.

We have fresh fruit and fish. We can help you ashore and find you a place to sleep that doesn't rock back and forth all night!"

Henry looked optimistic and wiped his eyes.

Perry wanted a bath and a chance to clean his clothing.

"What do you say, *Monsieur le capitaine?*" The fisherman had not changed his position and had now folded his arms.

"Let's see what we can figure out," said Capt. Dean.

It was at that moment that Perry finally realized that Captain Dean was totally out of his depth and as freaked out as he and Henry were about all of this.

"Where can we put in?" he asked. The man motioned to another nearby boat that was built with virtually no freeboard--so the sides of the boat were just inches above the surface of the sea.

They paddled into the shelter of the harbor and led them to a spot near a beach.

"Four fathom," said the short brown youth. His bronze skin and muscular torso showed that his life was one of hard work under the sun. He was the exact opposite of the English governor of the Virgin Islands.

Perry dropped the anchor and the engine was silenced.

"Why didn't they say anything about the motor and propellers, Captain?" said Henry.

"Maybe they were in awe about how we could move through the water without sails or paddles," suggested Capt. Dean.

"Like how we see UFOs, Henry," said Perry helpfully. "No idea how they are powered for interstellar space travel—we just know they can do it!"

Henry smiled for the first time in ages at the mention of UFOs since they both had had some interesting experiences recently in that department[ᵛ].

***

"What does *this* do?" The man was turning a can opener over and upside down.

Captain Dean demonstrated on a can of peas.

"How do you get the peas in the can?" the man asked.

The crew of the *Mary Celeste* found it challenging to explain modern things like a can of peas to people who lived three centuries in the past!

The one that really got them was the cigarette lighters. Instant fire—day or night. So cheap in Florida you could buy a dozen for ten bucks.

But here—in 1691—they were worth the equivalent of a gold ingot to these poor fisherman

---

ᵛ See: *Perry Normal & The Moons of Saturn*

and farmers living on the slopes of a slumbering volcano.

The fishermen on the dock really appreciated the heavy-duty black garbage bags—again, an everyday thing for Americans—a marvel for the natives.

To keep the bilge pumps working and to keep the sludge in the diesel engines from gumming up the cylinders and moving motor parts, Captain Dean suggested they take her out 'for a spin' just beyond the reef in open water.

The reef was the unspoken limit for most native boats since the water often dropped off too deep for seaweed and other food that fish eat.

Most fishing was done within two hundred yards of the shore. Sharks never came inside the reef anyways and that was a bonus.

But suddenly two different things happened that—together--would change their lives in a profound way.

The first was that the engines sputtered and died as the last of the fuel was sucked into the carburetor.

That meant that they were at the mercy of the current--which was strong off the Windward Islands running all the way down to Trinidad and Tobago.

Without power--they were a floating bathtub, a sitting duck.

The second thing that happened was the arrival of *The Dragon's Breath*—a sailing vessel slightly longer and wider than theirs and fully manned with dangerous pirates.

All they could do now was watch them pull alongside to check them out.

CHAPTER THREE   THE CAPTURE

Her captain stood on the poop deck aft--near the wheel, where he could get a good look at this pitiful little ship floating in the middle of nowhere.

"Speak!" he commanded to the huddled crew of the poor *Mary Celeste* now drifting helplessly.

"Ahoy, captain," said Capt. Dean, rising up as tall as he could make himself.   "How's your day going?"

"There's no masts, no spars, Captain," said one.

"There's neither sheets nor sails," said another.

"And what would you be doing out here, I wonder," said the pirate captain tucking his long red hair under his three-corner hat.

"Waiting for us to jiz come along," said another frightening face--leering from a cannon port.

"We're lost!" Perry stepped up to the rail and spoke to the captain.

"Lost? This is a bad place in the world to be lost, young jack," he said.

"Perry. It's Perry. My name. That's Henry, and that's Captain Dean."

"*Captain*? Have we ever seen a sorrier bunch of sailors? They couldn't fight their way out of a gunny sack! Hardy-har-har!"

The bearded pirate with a patch over one eye was laughing in their faces.

Henry heard Perry mutter: 'How would you know when you only have one eye to see with, stupid!'

Luckily, the words did not carry far.

"Well shipmates, you were *lost* but now you're *found!*"

The captain ordered men to board the stricken dive boat and bring the three castaways aboard his own ship.

Then he gave the order to strip the boat of anything that would be conceivably useful.

But that wasn't the worst!

The first mate Bunt—after seeing the *Marie Celeste* scavenged right down to her paintwork—ordered it to be burned.

Hungry orange flames licked at her decks and rails; the bridge collapsed in a shower of sparks. Inside of twenty minutes the *Marie Celeste* was no more!

"Take them below," ordered the captain.

Night--darker than dark--fell on the three prisoners in the lowest bowels of the pirate ship *The Dragon's Breath!*

***

Morning came to the salty Caribbean and the rolling pirate vessel and the boys blinked and sneezed as they came topside from below decks.

Being a frigate, *The Dragon's Breath* had a main deck and a lower berth deck which housed cannon which protruded through portholes on each side of the hull—twenty-two in all.

Perry sometime later asked the captain why 22; he said it's his lucky number.

You talk about 'luck', thought Perry. What kind of bad luck got us here as captives on a pirate ship?

As if to answer his question, Captain Bonney stepped down from the quarterdeck with a lively step and greeting:

"You are lucky to be alive. The sea is no friend to men in a boat with no sails and the lines of a bathtub." The pirate captain had a wicked twinkle in his eye.

"In any case, you're mine now, *my* crew—and you'll do as I command. Are we clear?"

"Yes sir!" said Perry and Henry together. Capt. Dean just nodded forlornly.

"We are Jamaica-bound, although of course we may spot a prize anywhere in these waters," Capt. Bonney went on.

"Can you work?" said Bonney.

The boys said they could.

"Can you fight?"

Capt. Bonney said taking a stride toward them with his hand on the pommel of a cutlass with a nasty blade.

"What choice do we have?" interjected Capt. Dean.

"None," said Bonney firmly.

"When we are taking a prize, we fight together— like the fingers of a fist. Every man attacks like a tiger. And every man shares equally in the spoils."

At this remark, a dozen pirates shouted "Aye!" and raised their hands in the air.

"We live together, we fight together, we drink together—and we die together!" the captain said.

His men cheered and pounded their fists on the rail.

"I run a tight ship—orderly and trim. Every man shall keep himself and his quarters clean and each takes responsibility for the ship.

Every day we undertake repairs, inspect the sails and rigging, polish the cannon, clean the muskets. The boatswain is your master during that time; then he reports to me.

I'll not tolerate ill behavior or fighting amongst yourselves.

We are men of honor and do not inflict unjust cruelty or harm upon our adversaries. We do not ravish or rape women, we do not take what is not rightfully ours.

We show respect whilst on shore and pay a fair price for lodgings, food and drink. We have letters of marque from His Majesty and give him his share of tax paid to local English authority—the Governor in Jamaica.

Punishment for not adhering to our rules is severe. You shall be flogged, or if need be—hanged."

Henry instinctively rubbed his neck as if an invisible rope were chafing him.

Perry—as usual—was not shy and was always curious, so he stood and spoke directly to the Captain.

"Captain Bonney, sir. Henry and I respectfully request to be apprenticed under your command. I believe we can prove to be of use.

Henry and I have training in the use of firearms, for example. I have knowledge that may persuade you to accept our loyal service. Sir."

Henry blanched. Captain Dean laughed into his sleeve. He was acting strangely lately.

"Come here, boy," said Bonney. "What is that thing in your hand?"

Perry had drawn his backpacker's compass from his front pocket and now thrust his hand out to meet that of the Captain.

"Sir. This is a compass. This will give us guidance as to the direction of North—no matter where we stand or sail. Look!"

Bonney leaned over the shiny device he was holding with a look of amazement.

"How came ye by this instrument, lad?" he said.

"I...ah...traded for it, sir. An old seadog came to have it, and in turn—it became mine." Perry could fake it like the best of them.

"Well, well, well—there's more to you than meets the eye, young Perry!" the Captain said heartily.

"Come show me how to use it; we are still days out from Port Royal and in excellent weather."

And with that, Perry and Captain Bonney traipsed to the foredeck--chatting like old chums.

"What do *we* do, Capt. Dean?" said Henry.

"Grab a cloth, Henry. Let's make like we're polishing *something*—a cannon, the rail."

"Can I say something, Capt. Dean?" said Henry.

"Have you looked in the mirror lately?"

"Why, no. Why do you ask, Henry?"

"You don't look like the captain we left Lauderdale with. Your hair! Your beard! They went from white to brown.

And you've shrunk! You look like a man under a spell—you are reverse aging, Capt. Dean! You look years younger--younger than my Dad!"

"Something must have happened to me going through the time-slip in the Triangle. I *feel* about forty years younger," he said.

"I am 74 years old, Henry, but I have the energy and zip of a thirty-year-old."

"You're freaking me out, Captain Dean. We hardly recognize you. You've morphed in just a few days into a completely different 'Thom Dean'.

You're not going to keep regressing I hope. I don't want to have to babysit you or change your diapers," Henry winked.

"We'll see, won't we Henry!"

And a much younger, happier Captain Dean lifted his feet in an Irish jig and twirled in a circle right there on the deck of the pirate ship *The Dragon's Breath.*

Chapter Four   Meet The Family

The next morning was a parade—a military term for gathering the men on deck for inspection.

Captain Bonney looked splendid in his deep navy blue waistcoat.

"Now that you are part of our crew, I believe you should know your shipmates, boys.

Our first mate—we call him Quartermaster—is Flingel Bunt who--having escaped His Majesty's Royal Navy--happily serves on our ship as my second-in-command.

He is in charge of distributing food and rum rations, assigning work, and--doling out punishment.

His favorite task is leading a boarding party when we attack a tempting prize at sea.

I've personally seen him sharpen a sword between some Spanish sailor's teeth. He calls it 'flossing', I don't know why."

Quartermaster Bunt stood about six foot three and weighed as much as a barrel of brandy, full. His smile was meant to be friendly, but the impression Henry got was this man should be obeyed at all costs.

"Now here's our boatswain--Mad Dog McGuinty. Don't ever cross him or try to fool him. He'll make you walk the plank. No blindfold.

He plans the day's work and sees to it that it gets done, if you take my meaning."

Perry and Henry nodded vigorously.

"Where would we be without a skilled helmsman; meet our sailing master McComb--we call him 'The Pilot'. No one knows his first name or if he even has one. He keeps to himself mostly.

His assistant navigator is Denté Fettuccine--who swears he is a direct descendent of Christopher Columbus--which I rather doubt. The name is Italian sounding, but..."

Bonney tugged affectionately on the shoulder of a burly bearded giant named Pistoff.

"A Russian on the run from the Czar we're told.

He's our Master Gunner and is a superb shot with cannon, of which we have twenty-two, as you know. Pistoff likes to make a lot of noise in battle. You will be his powder monkeys, Perry and Henry! He'll keep you busy!"

Pistoff spat out a word that sounded like a combination of 'greetings' in Russian, and 'I have a bad headache'.

"Did he say 'Arrghh!!" Henry whispered to Perry.

"Arrrghh!" said Perry with a grin.

"I didn't think pirates really said stuff like that," said Henry.

"Now boys—meet our buccaneers who will fight anyone anywhere--over anything!"

Bonney swept his arm wide in a welcoming gesture in the direction of some of the dirtiest, grimiest, nastiest men they could ever imagine.

"Ogultan is—*was*—a Turk fighting with the Barbary pirates off Libya. He was captured by the Spanish and forced to work on a slave ship down Africa way.

He *hates* Spaniards. You don't wanna know what he does when he boards a Spanish galleon. It involves a lot of blood.

Over here is Slash—good with a cutlass. Enough said."

He pointed to a skinny boy of no more than seventeen who was sitting in the rigging and waved and grinned at Perry and Henry. Then he made a screech like a seagull--which startled the tabby cat he was stroking.

"That's Birdy. He stays way up there in the crows-nest most of the day. Often sleeps up there with his cat, Tom. He is very good with ropes and knots and has sharp eyes when he's on lookout."

A muscular black man with an enormous laugh bowed to them. He had the look of a man who had spent a life in hard labor.

"That's Ohman. He's an escaped African slave. He's gawd-awful strong; he twisted and bent his own iron collar and ankle shackles off *himself.* That's why the scars."

Perry could see a white line across his throat where the cruel band had been fastened.

"We don't know if he speaks—all he says from time to time is "Oh! Man!" if there's a problem he has to deal with.

He works with the Petty Officer who's our rope and sailmaker. Another refugee from the Royal Navy. Things must be bad in the service if such men jump ship and join a band of pirates."

"Wha' about me, Cap'n?" said one of the smelly ones.

"That's Stinker," said Bonney with his nose wrinkled. "You can smell him even after he's dipped in the sea.

He's an Ordinary Seaman who has jobs such as cleaning the latrine, taking out the garbage, and swabbing the decks."

"Some'ns gotta do it," said Stinker.

"Aye, true enough," said Bonney stepping back a pace from the odorous seaman.

"You'll enjoy the fine French cuisine prepared by the Marquis de Montréal who drank himself into debtor's prison—but then escaped to sea. He's fashioned a little oven below decks that burns coal and so he turns out pastry for our men."

"*Monsieur Le Marquis*," said Bonney with a slight bow to the Frenchman--who was beaming with happiness and twirling his long moustache.

"He is ably assisted by those twins there: Postage and Handling, who assist with the cooking and cleanup and order provisions when we are in port. They are Jamaicans who fled the sugar plantations and have served us well.

Have I forgotten anyone?

Ah yes, our Chinese merchants Ming and Tian. They came to Jamaica to cultivate pearls and built a substantial trade hereabouts. They were accused of cheating their customers and were driven out—right into our waiting arms. Pearls are specially prized and worth as much as gold in the Caribbean."

"Enough o' this kissing 'n huggin'," shouted Mad Dog. "There's a ton o' work t' be done. You boys—go with the carpenter there and see what he needs.

"Mister…" McGuinty started to say, but Capt. Dean cut him off.

"It's *Captain* Dean."

"Not on this ship, it ain't! There's only *one* captain and his orders is the rules of this here vessel.

Now get yer sorry ass up that mast and give Birdy a hand with the rigging."

Captain Dean was surprised to find that climbing the rigging was a breeze. He had not had this kind of ability for many years.

The wind caught his hair and he shouted for sheer delight. After all, he *was* a sailor—muscle and bone, heart and soul—a man of the sea.

***

"Captain Bonney said this ship is a 'frigate'. How is that different from British or French warships?"

Perry was full of questions for Jim Beam—the chief carpenter on *The Dragon's Breath.*

"Frigates are smaller than ships of the line—the man o'war—and that makes 'em faster. Remember boys—speed and maneuverability are the keys to winning or losing at sea. Whether yer engaged in battle or running cargo, the fast ship wins.

If ye're merchant marine, your backers will pay you handsome if you get your cargo to port on time or ahead of time.

Now, mind—a frigate is a formidable piece of work; she's fifty tons of oak near eighty feet long and half as wide, carries up to 150 men and 36 guns and can run with the wind up to eight knots!"

Jim was warming to the topic of conversation. He loved this ship.

"This here vessel was a Dutch ship taken as a prize and refitted with better guns—ask Pistoff about that—and her decks and galley were re-planked and caulked to make her like new.

She's full rigged with three masts and cross spars and an easy two miles of rope and enough sail to cover half of Portsmouth. That's why we got a petty officer—least that's what the Navy would call 'im—to manage all that.

But there's a'plenty to do with the carpentry work, especially after we've been in a scrap and taken fire from cannon and musket ball.

You've no idea how hard it is to repair a hole in the hull below the waterline. Has to be done from the outside *in*, meaning you're gonna get wet and cold and maybe drownded—that's what happened to one of my apprentices. Swept clean away by a heavy sea.

Pity! We lost some good oak lumber along with him."

Perry and Henry liked Jim; he had a kindly face and rough hands that knew how to work wood with the few basic tools he had: plane, drill, adze, file, saw, hammer. Both Henry and Perry were eager to learn some useful woodworking skills from this man.

"Lemme show you the bowsprit—made it myself out of a single piece of ash wood. Had to use my imagination to carve a dragon's head; made it somewhat like the old Viking boats that had the same.

The bow of sailing ships need a reinforcing beam extending from the foredeck to support the jib sheets," he explained with pride. His handiwork was thrust forward boldly for all to see.

Their musing was interrupted by a shrill whistle from Quartermaster Bunt, summoning them to the main deck.

"What for?" asked Henry.

"Exercise period, lad," said Jim, looking a little perturbed.

Sure enough! It was like a crazy gym for pirates!

Each man spread himself out on the deck and the bos'n Mad Dog barked commands.

"Stretching....hamstrings. Relax the spine. Sink into the posture. Now—flip! Pull lower leg to buttocks and feel the stretch in your quads.

Good. Now sit-ups. Fifty, then lay back, then fifty more. Look lively now. Captain's coming!"

"G'day shipmates! Let's put our heart into it. A healthy crew is a happy crew!" said Capt. Bonney.

Push-ups, pull-ups, sit-ups, jumping jacks—the ship's crew were enthusiastically performing like the Brackendale gymnastics team--with one big exception. They were a ragtag band of filthy, smelly pirates and they were singing sea shanties!

Even Perry and Henry knew the words!

What shall we do with the drunken sailor? What shall we do with the drunken sailor? What shall we do with the drunken sayy-lor...er-lye in the morn'in!"

All the while the cooks had been slaving over the hot stove stirring huge pots of barley and oat porridge they called *burgoo,* and frying fatty wads of preserved pork, accompanied by white beans stewed in sweet molasses with a hint of rum, and all served with hunks of fresh French bread.

The galley was on the lower deck where the men slept and most of the supplies including gunpowder were kept.

That would explain the no-smoking rule that Mad Dog strictly enforced below decks.

Somehow they had room for oaken tables and benches and the whole noisy boisterous bunch of them chowed down on the best breakfast to be found anywhere at sea!

Perry murmured to Henry.

"If this is a pirate's life, it's not bad at all!"

"We haven't seen the worst part yet, Perry. We haven't had to fight and kill people, we haven't been seasick or swamped by a hurricane. But you are right—the food is pretty darn good!"

Jim Beam slopped more food onto their plates.

"Eat up boys while the eatin's good!"

Chapter Five   Be Careful What You Wish For

"Henry, what are we going to do? We have slipped back in Time and there's no guessing how or *if* we can ever get back to our own time and our own families!"

Perry was clearly upset because he was wringing his hands—something Henry had never seen Perry do before.

"*You* kept wishing you could be a pirate! Remember Henry? And here you *are*—a pirate, or a pirate-in-training. Did you have to drag the rest of us along with you?"

"Chill, Perry. We'll get out of it—we always do. Whatever strange forces pulled us back to 1691 will surely release us once again to the 21st Century.

You believe as much as I do that everything happens for a reason.

And yes, I wanted to experience the real, genuine pirate experience—like most kids do.

It's funny—why do kids who grow up in affluence fantasize about being buccaneers? It's like we want to be free of parents and teachers and all their rules. Just like pirates are."

"Well, we have movies to carry us away to distant times and places; it's a whole other thing when it happens for real," said Perry.

I never told anyone how deeply affected I was by my time-slips to Santorini or Rome. How could I?

First of all, nobody would believe me except you. Professor Wegener thought I was a nut-case.

Time travel sounds cool—until you try it. Since there is no user's manual on 'Time Travel', no one is prepared for the 'side effects', shall we say.

And when we return to normal life, the adjustment is a killer. You're going to find that out yourself if we are fortunate enough to find a way home again."

At that moment, the breeze picked up and the sails billowed—ropes straining and creaking.

"Look lively, boys," said the bosun. "We've caught the tradewinds that'll carry us home."

Perry muttered in a low voice.

"Not the home I want to go to."

***

"Hey Perry, I have an idea. Two ideas actually.

First of all, we know more geography than the Kings of Europe! More than the navigators on any ship of the 17ᵗʰ Century. One of the ways we could avoid all the climbing and lifting is to use our natural intelligence!

I mean, why don't we approach Capt. Bonney and tell him what we know about the Caribbean, the United States, South America and the secret that Panama is hiding—easy access to the Pacific?"

"What proof do we have, Henry? What are we going to say—we are time-travellers from the future who know the world better than he ever will?"

"That's a good point, Perry. Maybe we could say we have lots of sailing experience...". Henry's voice trailed off.

"Sure. In a small fishing boat with no sails or rudder found floating in the middle of nowhere. I don't think so, Henry!"

"Okay, Perry. Let's try it this way. We tell him and sketch it out for him to show that we know the placement and relative position of every place that touches the Caribbean Sea. From Florida to Cartagena. Fill in the map in a way that will convince him!

Never mind *how* we know—we *know*. Knowledge is power, Perry, as you have often said. Let's use that knowledge to buy safe passage on this floating circus."

"Now you're talking, Henry!" Perry brightened up at once.

"Mr. Bunt, sir. We would respectfully ask to have a word with Capt. Bonney." The two boys stood straight and tall on the quarterdeck.

"It's good ye show respect when talkin' to a superior officer," First Mate Bunt replied.

"It starts with respect. Respect leads to order. Order leads to efficiency. Efficiency leads to...".

"Success!" Perry finished the sentence that the quartermaster could not.

"Aye! Success! Clever lad! Now come this way."

No man but Bunt had been inside the captain's private apartment below the quarterdeck. It was naturally off-limits to the crew. Even in port, no one could be seen in that part of the ship without good reason.

"Our two castaways would be wanting a chat with ye, Captain," Bunt announced through the heavy door.

"Aye sir," said Bunt.

"Slip off your shoes and speak clearly as to yer purpose when ye goes in. If he offers ye drink— never refuse." He winked and slipped back up the hatchway. Perry turned the iron handle and pushed on the stout oaken door.

"Come—sit. I am still toying with that little compass you gave me. I'm amazed it works at sea; I had heard explorers and such use this tool on land.

So what have you got for me today, my boys!"

"We need chart paper and a pencil, Captain." Perry moved to the table littered with bread crusts and soup stains on various papers covered with the captain's scribbles.

"Sir? What if I told you that Henry and I had knowledge that would be of tremendous value to you in your navigation about the Caribbean?"

Without waiting for an answer, Perry—in conversation with Henry—sketched a quite accurate depiction of the whole of Central America from 30° North latitude to 10° North latitude.

In short—from Louisiana to Colombia.

The whole sweep of the Gulf of Mexico appeared as if by magic from Perry's pencil. The isthmus of Panama, the coastline of Colombia and Venezuela all the way to Trinidad-Tobago.

And it was more or less to scale.

Perry started to fill in the islands: Cuba, Jamaica, the Dominican Republic, Puerto Rico.

The Captain grew anxious for some reason.

"Exactly how came you to have this information?" he blurted out finally.

"There is no man alive that knows this; how did two young lads come to be so skillfully trained in the arts of mapmaking?"

A cloud threw shade on the room and the voice of the captain grew threatening.

"Are you sorcerers? Magicians? Students of the Dark Arts? Tell me quick!"

"We are travellers from a land where many things are known, yet are hidden," said Perry artfully.

It is your good fortune, Captain, that Henry and I were brought by Divine Providence to your doorstep—ah, ship-step...or whatever."

Now Henry started.

"Yeah, Captain, sir. Our mission is to share this information with those who are worthy, and so allow us your kind hospitality while we explain all that has been written on this map. Sir."

The captain's jaw was open and he was breathing heavily.

"Rum! I need rum!" He dashed to his cupboard and pulled out a bottle and three glasses.

He poured it out and gulped his down in a hurry.

"Drink up, lads. This is Jamaican rum and there's none finer in all the Seven Seas."

Perry looked at Henry and winked. They took a sip. Henry choked and coughed, and Perry winced as the fire burned all the way down.

"Arrghh!" said Captain Bonney.

Perry realized at last how this pirate expostulation could mean many things—depending on context.

Perry continued his lesson.

He penciled in the vast arc of islands in the eastern Caribbean from Trinidad up to Barbados and St. Lucia to the Bahamas. His memory was very good.

All Captain Bonney could do is stare in amazement, sipping rum and muttering under his breath.

"We are *here*," said Perry, showing a westerly course inbound to Jamaica. His map showed the proportional sizes and distances correctly.

"If we log the approximate speed of the ship with the estimated distance left to Port Royal, we can find the time left on our voyage. That can help estimate the food and water consumption more accurately.

Which, in turn, will make future voyages easier in terms of stocking the ship with supplies. Which means we won't carry any more cargo than necessary, so we can run faster..."

The captain cut him off excitedly.

"And catch our prizes more easily because they will not be able to outrun us!"

The captain leaped to his feet, spilling a drop or two of gold liquid onto the surface of the map.

"I am constrained to say that you are two remarkable fellows, and your knowledge has saved me years of bashing about this 'Spanish Lake' 's wot the Spanish governor in Cartagena calls it.

Now I can *plan* expeditions using...what did you call it? 'Scientific' principle--instead of guesswork!

You won't breathe a word of this to The Pilot, will you?" Captain Bonney's brow was furrowed.

"This is strictly between us three, Captain," said Perry, leaning toward the captain, dropping his voice to nearly a whisper.

***

"Perry? Here is my second idea."

Henry was standing on deck sniffing the fresh morning breeze that lifted the sails and the spirits of sailors.

"We have the benefit of all the scientific knowledge developed from 1700 to 2018. We know what Darwin and Mendel and Linnaeus developed in biology, and why it was so enormously important to Science.

Why don't we tear a page from their journals of discovery? Why don't we start documenting the flora and fauna of every place we land up? Like Darwin did while sailing on the good ship *Beagle* to the coast of South America and the Galapagos Islands?

Hey! We might even discover something Darwin overlooked. We can use the classifications of species and types given in the official taxonomies of organisms."

"Sure," said Perry enthusiastically. "Let's include marine organisms and birds. I've never seen so many birds and their behavior is remarkable.

I saw Birdy up in the crows-nest feeding several; I don't know how he got them to trust him enough to land up there, but he did! Even with a cat!"

So Perry Normal, Junior Scientist from Brackendale, New York, and his friend and colleague—Henry Schuyler--began a new kind of activity that was not too common among pirates—the study of Nature and her wonders.

CHAPTER SIX   THE CAPTAIN RULES!

On every ship the Captain is the commander—
whether you are under the British flag, or some other.
Like the Jolly Roger.

The legendary pirate flag has been seen in red or
in black—but always with some grim symbols of
Death and Retribution. Blackbeard's ship was called
Queen Anne's Revenge and no pirate was more
feared in his time than William Teach and his beard
of twisted hair and hemp that gave him his nickname.
His flag was blood red with a depiction of the violence
he was known for.

The Dragon's Breath had such a flag of black with
skull and crossbones to announce her intentions.

If it became tattered or torn, it was dutifully taken
down and mended by hand—just as sails were.

At times it would be furled on deck and in the heat
of attack be raised to the horror of the victims who
now knew their demise was at hand.

Let it be said as well, however, that *discipline* was a
basic principle of any well-managed vessel. *The
Dragon's Breath* was no exception.

The usual routines and schedules of ship maintenance and operation were in place. But Captain Bonney had added a twist of his own to shipboard routines.

Like exercise. There was a rare day when the bosun didn't have the men up early on deck— stretching and flexing, rolling on their backs with knees clasped to chest.

"For your spine," he said. "A flexible spine is the key to physical and mental health," Capt. Bonney often said.

Which is why—one sunny day—he himself got up on the quarterdeck just in a short sleeve shirt, and began a new series of exercises.

None of the men would ever learn that Perry and Henry had not only committed to augmenting the exercise program, but had agreed to train Capt. Bonney in some basic yoga postures—'for the spine'.

"Now lay down with hands under your chest and slowly curl up—like a cobra—and hold for twenty seconds. Good. Now let yourself reverse that slowly until your face is on the deck once more."

Seventeen men and three captives now got on hands and knees to perform the Cat Pose, the Dog

Pose, the Triangle Pose, and finished with the Vow to the Sun pose.

Capt. Bonney was beaming with delight.

Then the bosun took them through the usual running in place and jumping jacks.

Along with occasional fasting on vinegar and water, these sailors were not gaining any weight.

"Haven't felt this good in years," Captain Dean said.

Both Captains were wise enough to know that keeping busy and fit were excellent ways to make the miles pass at sea.

Since the map lesson, Captain Bonney had infinitely more regard for the two boys.

So when they suggested beefing up the exercise program, he was quite willing to listen.

Henry had a black belt in martial arts—something he kept quiet at school about, but which was now going to make him a pirate superstar!

**

The morning warmups were complete. The bosun Mad Dog McGuinty sat on the gunwale and watched as Henry placed the crew in two wide rows in front of him.

"There are two basic skills in fighting with bare hands," Henry began.

There was some murmuring about '*why bare hands when there are plenty of weapons about?*'

Henry continued.

"One is *offence*; one is *defense*." Each requires different movements of the hands, arms, torso and legs. We train so that these become automatic. In battle, as you must know, there is no time to think—only react. You must react correctly or it may cost you!"

Henry was a sight to see, Perry was thinking. He was so proud of his longtime friend.

"Always start with whatever the moment calls for.

Stinky—will you come up please?

Now...take a swing at me."

Stinky launched a right hook and Henry blocked it with his left hand, sliding over Stinky's arm like a snake—a move which deflected the blow away.

Then Henry surprised them all by seizing that incoming punch with the blocking hand, pulling Stinky a foot forward and off-balance—and countering with a deft punch with his own right hand to the chin—sending Stinky sprawling on his back.

The men clapped and Stinky sat up wondering what had hit him.

"So this is how a defensive move flips into an offensive move that gives you swift advantage over your opponent."

Henry then drilled them in punching effectively from the waist, kicking at knee or groin height, stepping in to attack and stepping out to avoid attack.

He showed them how to use palm and elbow strikes from any position.

He showed basic blocks with palms and arms.

He would have gone on all morning except that Bos'n McGuinty hollered it was time to do their duties regarding ship maintenance.

Henry was covered with beads of sweat on his face and neck when he finally collapsed on the bench beside Perry.

"I would kill for a hot shower," he admitted.

"Totally hear you!" said Perry. "Are you going to do this every day?"

"Alternate days for martial arts. I have another trick up my sleeve for tomorrow," Henry said with a grin.

"Do tell," said Perry.

"Actually, I will need your help. This will involve teamwork. I will tell you at breakfast, which I sincerely hope will be soon!"

***

By having the two Brackendale boys infuse the morning programs with new energy and ideas, Captain Bonney could devote his time to planning his next three months of pirating: go to Jamaica for R&R, capture any foolish ships that crossed his path, make any repairs to the ship that might be needed.

In his mind, pirating was like any other business enterprise—maximize opportunities for profit, and minimize risks and damage. Simple.

Which made the program for today quite amusing, but quite relevant for this seagoing CEO.

Henry and Perry had organized what they called a 'staff development seminar' along the lines of what a marketing department might do to improve sales performance.

First, the crew would pair off with a partner, then introduce themselves and share a personal anecdote or favorite moment.

This would take about ten minutes. Then Perry stood up, welcomed them, and said:

"We want to build your skills as a buccaneer. Yesterday Henry showed you hand-to-hand combat skills; today we want to show you interpersonal skills that include communication that is more effective."

All eyes were on Perry although many shook their heads as if trying to eject a bee that had flown into their ear canal.

"Our first scenario," said Henry, rising to his feet and strolling among the men on deck, "is to learn to show your partner and crewmate *support*. For example, you show your care and attention by being polite when speaking.

You might say to your partner: 'How is your day going?' or 'What do you need in your life right now?'.

Let them respond while you use body language like smiling and nodding to indicate you are listening to them in a caring way."

Slash was muttering, so Henry turned to him and asked him to stand up, which he did in a blushing awkward kind of way.

Henry rested his hand on Slash's upper arm near the shoulder and said: "Slash? How can I help you be a better pirate today?"

Henry was smiling and touching Slash and Slash was squirming like a rabbit someone had picked up by the ears.

"Ahhh, gimme twice the helpings at lunch than I usually get," he said with a grin.

"You see, everyone? Slash is opening up and sharing his hidden needs, which makes him easier to work with and understand. He's human—like all of us. And he needs to know that someone cares.

You may sit down, Slash," said Henry soothingly.

Slash looked like a bird that had flown into a window—temporarily stunned.

"Let's take ten minutes and practice this idea of being supportive with your words and body language."

To Captain Bonney's amusement—they did. There was more conversation between his men that there had been since their last shore leave.

Ming and Tian were paired up with McComb and Denté. They got into a heated discussion about how to market pearls and the kinds of prices they might fetch.

The Turk and the Russian were arguing about whether vodka was better than rum and why Islam prohibited its followers from consuming either.

Postage and Handling were coaxing Capt. Dean to talk, while Birdy just pulled out a deck of cards and was dealing a hand for each of them. His cat Tom was licking his paws.

Bunt and McGuinty were passing a brown paper bag back and forth and appeared to be drinking something inside of it.

Their seniority over the crew allowed them privileges that might bend the rules from time to time.

'No drinking on the job' was a basic rule but the crew was having such a good time that no one noticed.

"They're having an authentic pirate encounter," Henry whispered to Perry.

"Where'd you learn all this terminology, Henry?"

"From my Mom. She goes to Human Potential workshops all the time and comes home happy for days."

"Cool!" said Perry. "What's next?"

Henry lay two fingers on his lower lip and whistled in a loud shrill.

"Okay, shipmates. Now we're going to change it up a bit. Each pair will role play so that one of you will be a pirate, and one of you will be a prisoner. The point being that we learn to treat prisoners with the same respect we ourselves would want."

He went over to Ogultan and asked:

"Ivan Pistoff is your captive. Ask him what he needs right now."

"What you are needing, you filthy Russian?

"Vodka," said Ivan.

"Ask him how you could make him more comfortable," Henry coaxed.

"Give me one good reason why I should not kill you right now?" said Ogultan in a reassuring voice.

"Try to put it in a more positive way, Ogultan."

"I hate people in general," he said—as everyone knew anyway.

"He's not a *real* captive—we are just playing make believe, if I could put it that way."

"Oh, okay," said Ogultan. "Let me try this one, Henry: 'How are the chains fitting you? Not too tight?'. How did I do, Henry?"

"Excellent, Ogultan. You see? Your mock prisoner feels so much better knowing that you care about him as a person, that you see him as a human being."

"Does everyone see my point here?" Henry added, looking around the deck at each one.

"Okay, now reverse roles. Again—as we saw with Ogultan and Pistoff—aim for a peaceful rapport with your prisoner.

Try not to use violence or even the threat of violence to make your point.

Persuasion using kindness can work to your advantage."

The Marquis jumped to his feet, bowing to his partner—in fact he bowed to everyone including Henry and Perry, saying: "I am zo zorry but I must go below to prepare zee lunch now. *Je comprend tout.* I realize now how important caring for others is. Zo, I will make a special surprise for za midday meal!"

"*Merci,*" said Mad Dog waving a hand still holding the paper bag.

"*Tres bien!*" said Bunt, reaching for McGuinty's outstretched hand.

"I am so proud of all of you," said Henry. "Perry and I are always here if you need someone to talk to or help you with your interpersonal skills."

"Aye! And so am I!" shouted McGuinty. "Now let's get some work done ere lunch!"

Men scrambled to find a rope to repair, a deck to mop, a bannister or railing to polish.

But the mood was uncharacteristically joyful, as if the men had come out hibernation into the pleasant sun of springtime.

Captain Bonney tipped his hat to the boys, who happily went below to help Ivan Pistoff--from Sant Pyotersboorg Rrrussia--count cannon balls.

A delicious smell wafted up from the galley where the Marquis was singing in French and chopping vegetables.

The sun was high over the yardarm when the meal call came.

PART II A Pirate's Life

Chapter Seven   Day In, Day Out

There are times at sea during rough weather or during battle when there is no time to think and barely time to act.

There are other times—like when you are becalmed or running before a light wind with nothing but oceans and seas all around—that you having nothing to do and must improvise.

Now Henry was a chess whiz; Perry could certainly play but it wasn't his favorite.

But desperate times call for desperate measures—and they were desperately bored right now.

The ship was barely moving on its course to Jamaica, there were no flying fish to chase, no whales spouting along side the ship—nothing, zero, nada.

So Henry and Perry made a chessboard from a piece of board, drew all the squares, and fashioned 'men' from wine corks, bits of metal like screws and nails—whatever was lying around loose and served the purpose.

Chess was a thinking person's game, so unfortunately pirates were not well suited to it. Pirates were men of action—not students in Middle School.

So when Perry and Henry sat down on their barrels which would serve as stools, the men gathered around—curious and interested.

"Iz like battle, no? Only vun vins," said Pistoff.

"Correct," said Henry. "Each piece is a man with certain power who can act for his own benefit, or act to defend his side," he explained.

"There are rules," Perry went on. "These rules are like the Rules of Engagement on a real battlefield.

For example, the Knight on his Horse—that's the brass button here—can move this way or that but only in that manner.

Once a piece makes contact and claims that space, the opposing player's piece is 'dead' and out of the game."

"And in the end? How does it end?" asked the twins Postage & Handling at the same time.

"When the King—that's the wine cork here—is under attack and cannot escape, and will therefore die. Chess players call that situation 'checkmate'," Henry said.

"Enough talk--play!" said Ogultan in a commanding voice.

Perry was white; he advanced his first pawn.

Henry moved his black pawn forward.

Perry moved another white pawn and a knight on his next move—and the game was going full throttle.

Birdy placed a bet on Henry. Slash bet on Perry.

Before you could say 'Check!' there was money being passed around and excited chatter in the circle of spectators.

Even Bosun McGuinty got in on the action and put five shillings on Henry—nearly a month's pay for a regular seaman!

Capt. Dean was too canny to bet on either boy—he knew the outcome would be very close; but of course, he knew these boys better than anyone.

In a certain way, Capt. Dean felt guilty for leading them away from port and into a wormhole that swept them all back in Time over three hundred years.

On the other hand, there would be no way to explain it to the police or the parents if they never returned to the future, to 2018, to the boathouse in Ft. Lauderdale.

That was in the hands of Fate, decided Capt. Dean. He hadn't asked to be here in 1691 but since he could do nothing about it, he decided to enjoy their little 'holiday' and worry about tomorrow—well, *tomorrow.*

"Checkmate!" announced Henry with glee.

That started a small riot on deck as men clapped each other on the shoulders while holding out their hands for payment.

Bosun McGuinty was first in line to collect from those who foolishly bet against him.

Every man on board knew that if McGuinty was in a good mood—they'd all have a nicer day.

But Perry was still twirling his thumbs.

"Henry? Did we salvage any fishing gear from the *Mary Celeste*? I have an idea!"

The four fishing rods were sturdy graphite composite rods made for marlin fishing.

They had a variety of hooks in the tackle box and plenty of line of different strengths.

They set up reels with 30-lb. test lines, attached hooks--and to the delight of their fellow crew--invited four of them to step up to the gunwale and try their luck.

This relatively modern approach to fishing was unknown to them.

Fishing traditionally was done with nets and sometimes gaffs—poles that ended in a nasty iron hook that was used at close range and required considerable skill.

The leisure lifestyle of later centuries would lead to sport fishing as a hobby. So these men were hugely entertained to have the opportunity to use a modern rod and reel.

Perry was helping two of them; Henry the other two. Again, a milling audience of sailors was pushing to get a view of the fishing line going over the side—with anticipation at what would happen next.

Of course, Henry had showed them how to cut bait and impale it on the hook and it got the best results.

Perry wanted to use a lure with flashing spoon and treble hook—this was what he preferred on fishing trips back in New York State, so he went with that.

The men didn't have to wait long for a strike!

Wham! A huge bluefin tuna nailed Ogultan's baited hook and—big and strong as he was—he had to haul hard on the line to get the monster up on deck.

The fish knocked over Birdy—who was skinny and weighed no more than one-twenty or so.

Everyone was laughing, and the twin cooks Postage and Handling dragged the flopping mass down the ladder to the galley, to be hacked into pieces and steamed for dinner.

The quartermaster Flingel Bunt was carefully coached by Perry to fling the line as far out as he could then slowly trawl it in—giving fish time to make up their minds to strike—or not.

A tug on the line made Bunt stagger—another monster fish—this time a red snapper of enormous size. Perry showed Bunt how to reel then wait, then reel like crazy until he got the fish up over the rail.

Again, the men were cheering and clapping. The Marquis claimed the fish for the Captain's meal that evening.

This business went on for an hour—tossing the line, reeling it slowly toward the hull of *The Dragon's Breath*—then repeating that until the line abruptly straightened and tugged on the rod, signaling another catch.

Perry got to explain to the men why the rod was so important. It was more than just a fishing pole, he said. It gave the fish resistance—tiring it out so it would lose its strength to fight.

There is an art to fishing, Perry explained.

After an hour of casting and hauling, they called it a day. Fresh fish for dinner made everyone have a good appetite.

Henry amazed them at dinner by explaining the nutritional value of protein and calcium from the fish meat—but lost them when he tried to talk about Vitamins A & D in the fish oil.

To be fair, Perry and Henry got a lesson as well when the main cooks: the Marquis de Montreal and Denté Fettucine showed them how fish is cut up and pickled in oak barrels filled with vinegar—or brine, if vinegar is not available.

Perry and Henry gabbed about salinity and pH the whole time, mystifying the cooks and intriguing Capt. Bonney--who had come down to have a look.

"You're providing useful amusement to my men," he said—obviously pleased.

"What else do you clever lads have up your sleeves?" the captain asked with a smile.

"One of our observations Captain Bonney is that there is no real provision for men who fall ill or suffer injury.

Henry and I propose to set up a 'sick bay' in some little corner of the lower deck--crowded though it is.

We have some medical training, you might say— what we call 'first aid'—to treat a man's wounds when they are fresh rather than when they have festered."

"Whatever you need, speak to Bunt. He'll open the cupboards for you boys.

I'm not sure how you came to be so wise at such a tender age, but I see Providence has seen fit to put you in my road—and I'll not forget it!"

With Captain Bonney's blessing, Perry and Henry organized a First Aid club with its very own sick bay in a storage area for powder and cannonballs.

"Let's discuss the most common injuries," said Henry.

"Broken bones for sure," said Perry.

"Right so we need splints and bandaging, maybe improvised crutches. We can get the wood from the carpenter Jim Beam."

"Cuts, scrapes, gashes—anything that causes bleeding or exposes the flesh to infection and loss of blood and lymphatic fluid," said Perry.

"Okay. More bandages and gauze patches.

And don't forget Perry—the basic rule of first aid is to treat shock from loss of lymph and blood by hydrating the individual and keeping them warm."

"So we need blankets. What about stretchers to get the injured below, out of the melee on deck?", suggested Perry.

"I would say 'yes' but how the heck are we going to get a 200-pound man on a stretcher down a small hatchway to sick bay?" Henry pointed out.

"That does pose a challenge, Henry. Let me think about that," Perry replied.

"What about disinfectants?" asked Henry.

"Well, we *do* have an abundance of alcohol—that rum the men are guzzling is at least 150 proof. Divide that by two and you get the percentage of alcohol in the liquid—which is otherwise mainly burnt sugar and water."

"Good enough," said Henry. "That's going to kill any bacteria pretty quickly. For treating topical abrasions and other unpleasant things like lice or skin issues like fungus or scabies we could try vinegar mixed with gunpowder or even strong black tea."

"Vinegar and gunpowder? Is this an old New York Dutch recipe? Where on earth would you get this idea?" said Perry in amazement.

"I'm not sure but I think the Continental Army during the War in 1778 had something like that. They certainly did *not* have penicillin and tetracycline.

It is worth a try!" Henry affirmed.

"So who is going to be in charge of the sick bay—us?" asked Perry.

"Until this ship gets a proper medic—I think it has to be us," said Henry.

"Besides," he added, "It sure beats lifting cannonballs and kegs of highly explosive gunpowder!"

Perry laughed.

"Yeah, you're right about that, Henry. Gives us an excuse to stay below while the real pirates like Slash and Ogultan give hell to the enemy from the main decks."

CHAPTER EIGHT   STAND & DELIVER!

'Red sky in the morning: sailors take a warning; red sky at night: sailor's delight' goes the old saying.

The next day dawned with a fierce crimson sunrise and a strong easterly breeze that smelled of salt and seaweed.

"Full moon means a change in the weather," said Capt. Dean pulling up a barrel to sit on.

"You mean a storm coming?" said Henry with some trepidation.

"Could be. The sky will cloud over and darken rapidly if that's the case. We've been lucky so far."

"Henry and I are missing our friends, our Malt Shop, and..."

"And the Internet!" said Henry. "I never realized being at sea could be so...*tedious*. That's a word our English teacher Mrs. Busby always uses.

Perry and I are doing everything we can think of to entertain ourselves but it's just not the same. I guess what I mean to say is that we are *homesick*. And what is the cure for that, Capt. Dean?"

The cure seemed to come out of nowhere as Birdy hollered down to the quartermaster: "Ship ahoy!"

Men slithered down ropes, appeared in hatchways, and the Captain appeared with a spyglass on the fore deck near the bow.

"I smell Spanish treasure," said Mad Dog sniffing the air like a dog would.

"Aye, I see the masts and hull looking very Spanish," said Bonney. "Let's get ready."

"Battle stay-shuuunns!" hollered the quartermaster Bunt. "Prepare to fire!"

Cannon were wheeled up to gun ports and charged with powder; balls were inserted in the muzzles and rammed down the barrel close to the breech where the powder charge was.

Blade weapons of various kinds--from curved cutlasses to thin Scottish dirks with long evil blades-- were passed out.

"We were trained last summer in *boot* camp," Henry reminded Perry, "but we did not train in hand to hand combat with weapons. We learned to shoot, sure, but didn't even get to practice with bayonets.

It's like it was all a theatre rehearsal—no one prepared us to *kill*, Perry!"

"I totally get where you're coming from, Henry. But we are *pirates* now and we have to be prepared to be as vicious and violent as the rest of them!

Think of all the young American boys who shipped out to Vietnam or Iraq or Afghanistan. They were just kids many of them."

The noise on deck signaled the approach of the target.

"Better get ready, Henry," said Perry—his face white and his voice shaking.

"Here, Henry. Take this." Perry handed Henry an unfinished table leg made of sturdy oak that he had scrounged from the carpenter's workshop.

He picked another piece of lumber that he could manage as a club and they both disappeared up the hatch.

***

The only things the boys knew about pirates came from movies or books—that included what they do when they encounter their intended prize.

So they did not know what to expect--except a lot of noise and commotion.

The reality was much worse!

Pirate tactics consisted of approaching a slower larger vessel, sneaking up alongside, then scaling the sides and viciously and aggressively attacking the enemy crew with sudden overwhelming force.

One thing could be said about Capt. William Bonney—he did not show any hesitation to do just that.

Perry and Henry helped get the longboats launched by lowering them on stout ropes to the water.

At the very moment the Spanish ship realized their danger, cannon from *The Dragon's Breath* tore into her sides and sheets—creating confusion and havoc as they tried to return fire.

Most of the men on the Spanish side were unprepared for being boarded, and few had muskets or pistols ready to shoot. By the time they did—it was too late!

Ogultan had their lieutenant by the throat, Slash cut his way along the main deck through screaming men, Birdy flew up the main mast and cut her rigging at critical points—causing the sails to slump on top of the deck and cover the Spanish crew.

Capt. Bonney spun a six-inch gun mounted on the poop deck, took aim, and fired at the wheel that the Spanish admiral was desperately trying to control.

Splinters of wood and of flesh and bone flew in all directions.

'Carnage' was the word Capt. Dean would later use when referring to the attack.

The two ships were now touching—starboard to port—as more pirates clambered over the downed sails and poured into the hold, looking for treasure.

A few Spaniards gained a hold by throwing a hook onto the gunwales of the pirate ship and pulled themselves up and over.

Henry immediately and without hesitation brained one with his club. Then another.

Perhaps they didn't see the smaller pirates amid the smoke and melee.

Perry had a sudden inspiration to yank the bucket from the latrine—which happened to be full and very nasty—and dump it and its contents onto the heads of two men just coming over the rail.

Covered in shit and piss—the two cried out, let go, and plunged fifteen feet to the sea below.

At length, the second-in-command on the Spanish ship cried: "We surrender!" and his men sat down on the deck—having thrown their weapons into a pile and awaiting their fate.

From below decks, the pirates emerged with barrels of good wine and meat—provisions for the long voyage across the Atlantic to Cadiz.

A goodly share of Spanish gold coins from Peru were retrieved, as well as silverware and goblets, candelabra and pieces of eight still attached in the form of small plates right from the furnaces.

The men made a relay with ropes so that these items could be ferried across the narrow gap separating the ships, and then Perry and Henry helped stow the booty below.

Capt. Bonney ordered the dozen females to be brought aboard and taken below. They were officer's wives and handmaids and were to be treated respectfully, he said.

Once the valuables had been taken off the Spanish vessel, she was torched.

This was the most disturbing part for the boys—because it had happened to them, and because there were still a hundred men on board who now had to throw themselves into shark-infested waters to escape being burned alive.

Perry was so upset that he confronted Capt. Bonney personally.

"They have clearly lost. Do they deserve to die in this cruel way?" he demanded of the pirate chief.

"This is how it's done, boy," said Bonney grimly. "Now get below and see to the prisoners!"

Perry did as he was told, but did not speak again to anyone that day—not even to Henry or Capt. Dean.

***

The next day was a day for dividing the spoils and Perry was to learn a peculiar aspect of pirate life: fairness.

Each man on board received an equal share of the booty, so each man was rewarded for the toil and blood spent to capture it.

Perry and Henry were smart enough to realize that to refuse was disrespectful and dishonorable both to the captain, and to the Pirate Code.

Among others—the Marquis was good at calculating the estimated worth of treasure—he had spent time in a French prison for his gambling and other debts.

"Think of this as a paycheck," whispered Capt. Dean as the coins and bullion were shared out.

He was grinning as they filled his hands with gold and silver--overlooking the price in human life that had been paid to get it.

So Perry filled his baseball cap with coins and Henry collected the same and put it in his waist-pouch, not at all used to having cash in its heaviest form.

The whole ceremony was concluded with a shot of rum seized in the raid. Mad Dog declared that such rum always tasted better and the men seemed to agree.

Perry was soon to learn the fate of the Spanish ladies who lay below on straw pallets—unchained and unharmed but in constant dread nevertheless.

The French colony of Haiti lay two days sail east of Jamaica. It was making plantation owners wealthy as the main money crop in the Caribbean shifted from tobacco to sugar.

Just off the north coast lay the small island of Tortuga—a favorite among pirates for various reasons.

First of all, it was somewhat sheltered and offered protection from hurricanes and storms.

It was also very convenient for buccaneers to intercept Spanish galleons laden with gold and jewels heading back to Spain along the north coast of the much larger island to the west: Cuba!

Cuba was the last port of call for all Spanish ships carrying treasure from the Americas to Europe.

The massive ships were heavy and ungainly— making easy targets for pirates whose loyalty was only to their own hideous black flag with its skull and crossbones.

The pirate flag promised only death to the unfortunate vessels that were unlucky enough to see it coming into their view.

Tortuga was a day's sail from Santiago de Cuba on the southeast coast of that enormous island.

Capt. Bonney knew that his fair-skinned ladies would fetch a nice ransom if returned to a Spanish port.

However, he also knew that he could trade them for useful things like food and supplies at Tortuga—and let some other resourceful traders carry the women back to Spanish territory—ones who did not sail under the black flag of piracy and therefore not likely to be shot out of the water by Spanish cannon.

With this in mind, he directed his navigator and quartermaster to make for Tortuga and then disappeared below.

Gossip on board said that Capt. Bonney did not take any of the ladies into his private quarters and this was thought queer.

In fact, it was rare to have women on board ship.

In the minds of sailors all over the world, having a woman on board was bad luck. Sailors were very superstitious and would never question such beliefs.

Which is why Bunt and McGuinty kept their hands off the Spanish señoritas.

Besides, they had a small sack of gold to rest their grizzled chins on. Much better from *their* point of view.

"Land ho!" hollered Birdy from his perch atop the mizzen-mast.

Sure enough, the blue hazy island had come into view and the men made ready to go ashore for the first time in a month.

It's ironic that men who spend their lives at sea will not spend much time ashore. Sailors will seek the familiarity of the ship instead. Maybe it's the rocking motion that lulls a man to sleep who cannot sleep in a bed that doesn't move.

The harbor was not crowded—only privateers and buccaneers put in here, certainly not respectable ships with honest men aboard.

The quartermaster and the captain led the Spanish ladies up onto deck and arranged for a wooden ramp to be hooked onto the gunwales on the port side—allowing them to step off the ship and down to the dock in relative ease.

Men there stared with envy, thinking those thoughts that men do, as the ladies were escorted into a cargo area and then to a *petit maison* where they would await a ship to take them to Cuba.

"Monsieur," said the man in charge, " do you object if I pay you in French francs--rather than British pounds or Spanish *reals*?"

"I'll take any money that is good," said Capt. Bonney, relieved to be free of his female captives.

He was surprised but not disappointed to be paid in banknotes with a dashing portrait of the King Louis on one side.

He folded them into a wad of bills and stuffed them into his waistcoat. Every man kept his money in a special place that was unique to him.

This payment belonged solely to the captain of *The Dragon's Breath.*

Men followed the order of the quartermaster—*work before pleasure.* If the men got into the liquor and the arms of a local beauty—nothing could be done in time to set sail in a day's time or so.

So they hefted burlap sacks of flour and sugar and all kinds of things that the crew would need at sea.

Perry and Henry tried their hand at persuading two fat pigs to go up the ramp and onto the deck—

but the pigs were stubborn and stronger than the boys expected.

Postage and Handling seized the animals by slipping a noose around their hairy pink necks and literally dragged them up the wooden slope and down the hatchway to where livestock were penned.

Being 'ordinary seamen', they helped with odd jobs of every kind and could not think of moving up to the rank of 'able seamen'—not on a pirate ship, and not in the Navy--without years of hard loyal service to whatever King they served.

While the captain was making a bundle unloading his ladies, Quartermaster Bunt was buying a slave who would be useful on the voyage to Jamaica, and who would be sold once they had arrived.

It is a peculiar fact of history that slaves from Africa could work hard in the intolerable heat and humidity of the Caribbean climate—which included American states of the Old South.

The original laborers who came as indentured 'servants' from the British Isles were not suited to the demands of picking cotton or tobacco, and certainly not the very hard work of cutting sugarcane.

Nor were the native American Indians of the United States or of Central America.

So this was the beginning of the Triangular Trade of the 17th and 18th Centuries that brought British metal and textile goods both to the English colonies in America and the Caribbean--in exchange for sugar and tobacco--while Africans sold into slavery went due west to the canefields and plantations of those who profited from them.

Chapter Nine   A Slave's Story

The man was not wearing manacles or bearing whip marks on his flesh; his black skin was glistening with sweat as he carried his share of the cargo up the gangway to *The Dragon's Breath*.

He spoke neither English nor French--despite the colonial presence of both in Africa.

The only words he would say from time to time were "Oh, man!" apparently as a reaction to his circumstances in life.

So his nickname became 'Ohman' and he grinned when you spoke it to him.

He was strong--with rippling muscles that showed he was used to hard work, and his teeth were white as whalebone.

He showed his gratitude to being away from the evil slave traders of Haiti by smiling and nodding and lifting enormous loads down into the hold below.

Perry and Henry took a liking to him right away. Perhaps it was his simple, child-like innocence that shone in his handsome face and gentle manner.

Perhaps it was his presence as another pirate captive whose life was no longer of his own choosing.

So it was with delight that—when Quartermaster Bunt said they were to train Ohman in his duties—the boys befriended a stranger with no friends, no family and a dim future.

Precisely their own position here--sailing to Jamaica--in the Year of our Lord, 1691.

As it turned out, Ohman knew enough English to at least listen and understand what was being said to him.

The boys showed him around the ship and he impressed them with his ability to quickly absorb information and make efforts to learn more.

For example, the boys were standing on the main deck and pointing up to the sky—where Birdy had his watchman's nest—and Ohman then pointed to the mast with a quizzical look, as if to say 'Can I climb?' to which the boys nodded in assent.

Like a squirrel he scurried up the pole—using the rigging as steps—and soon was nearly level with Birdy, who was as surprised as anyone.

Once there, Ohman began to scan the horizon in all directions as if he were getting his bearings.

All sailors and navigators use landmarks such as reefs and islands to roughly determine location at sea. Yet how had Ohman come to know that?

"Maybe on the long voyage from Africa?" said Henry dubiously.

"I think it is instinct," said Perry. "He knows he can see more if he is at a height—what puzzles me though is what is going through his mind.

Like—how is he processing what he is seeing and sensing? Is he constructing a mental map of his surroundings? Can he smell the scents of land-based vegetation on the wind?

He must be doing calculations of relative distance between islands since we just passed the western tip of Haiti running under a warm wind blowing off the land," he said.

"He must be homesick," said Henry. "Poor guy! He will never see his homeland again.

I wonder if he had a family? A wife and kids, a home in his village, a place in his community that were all erased the day they hauled him to the coast—and the waiting ships?"

"Like us?" asked Perry.

"I don't have a wife and kids," said Henry with a giggle.

Ohman—seeming satisfied—slipped down the mast using rigging for hand and footholds like he had been doing it all his life.

He landed with a thunk! Then looked at the boys as if to say: "That was cool! What's next?"

He was only allowed to see what they boys themselves could see, and could not wander unaccompanied until the bosun knew he could be trusted.

Today, potatoes and pork roast were on the menu. The two hogs that came aboard yesterday were today's treat—and the Frenchman knew just how to cook them to perfection, with a crispy crust on the roast that drove men crazy.

Ohman was peeling potatoes and the boys were washing them—all eighty of them!

Henry did a quick calculation: $80 \div 20 = 4$ spuds for every man. If the Marquis wanted to serve them in a more exotic way—say, scalloped potatoes *au gratin*—there would be slicing required in 3/8" slices (the Marquis said 5mm), which required another calculation by Henry.

Four potatoes, cleaned—sliced into an average number of slices of about eight—would entail 640 slices with a sharp knife in semi-darkness, as daylight seldom came down into the galley and candlelight was pitiful for such close work.

Luckily, Fettucine was the one selected to do this task—the Marquis could not trust anyone else to do it properly.

But Perry and Henry—once they were done washing and passing the potatoes to the Italian who was the Assistant Cook—got to fetch the hard cheese from the barrel and start to grate it into little piles around two inches in diameter, to go into the cheese sauce that would go onto the scalloped potatoes, to go into the bellies of twenty hungry pirates!

"We could spend out whole life down here preparing food," said Henry to Perry.

"Could be worse," said Perry. "We could have Stinky's job!"

"Speaking of which, where did you get the brilliant idea of dumping the bucket of shit on the Spanish sailors trying to board us?" said Henry.

"I couldn't think what to do!" said Perry. "I see two guys with knives in their teeth coming up ropes to board our ship and I had no weapon other than a hunk of lumber.

I don't have much experience hitting people with wood--but as I turned I saw the shit-hole that is used by people on the stern deck and I knew Stinky had not emptied it yet because he only did that in the mornings—so I drew out the bucket and gave the Spanish a good old American prank greeting!"

"I nearly died laughing," said Henry. "Can you do that again next time we're attacked and boarded?" he said.

"Depends on the time of day," retorted Perry. "Only works if the bucket is full!"

"Oh, man!" said Ohman.

"Must be getting tired of peeling," said Perry.

The Marquis said '*Merci*' to Ohman and the boys and dismissed them to the upper deck where they could get some air and taste the tropical breeze.

"Ohman," began Perry. "Will you tell us how you came to be on a slave-ship bound for the Americas?"

So Ohman told Perry and Henry the following story.

"I grew up in the small African country called Benin. My mother was from the Fon tribe and my father was from the Ibo tribe. These are the two dominant tribes in central west Africa and they are constantly in competition with other tribes like the Yoruba of Nigeria."

Oman shifted his weight on the sack of barley so he was more comfortable, then continued.

"There had been a slave trade for centuries in North Africa in Libya and Algeria and they prized European women who were desirable for harems and warlords--so had a brisk trade in the Mediterranean.

It was only when the Portuguese began to colonize The New World did anyone come to our lands to buy slaves. My people are hard workers and strong— which was exactly what the colonials in Central and South America were after.

It takes endurance to work in the hot humid climate—and work hard—planting, cutting, harvesting, and only the African can do this. The white man must hide in the shade of his hacienda and drink something cool. He will get the fever—and then a black man must bury him.

I was young and worked unloading cargo in Porto Novo—named by the Portuguese merchants who traded metal tools and cloth and glassware to Africans who did not have these things.

But we did not have banks or money; what could we exchange for these material advantages? Human lives!

A ship would arrive in port, offload its goods, and take a certain number of slaves in return. The local officials condoned this—they were paid off, you see!

My turn came. They said my parents will receive some gold and silver from the captain of the slave ship *Rio Negro* but I never knew if it were true. I hope so.

Many of my companions were prisoners of one kind or another; some were criminals and some—like me—were just men with no alternative but to be taken and hope Fate will be kind."

"How many men came with you?" asked Henry.

"There were a hundred of us—although I heard of ships from Nigeria taking over four hundred at a time. They went to Brazil and Cuba and anyplace in the Caribbean that needed cheap labor. I heard some went to a place called Carolina to grow tobacco or cotton."

"We've heard of that place too," said Perry, glancing at Henry, his voice tinged with irony.

Ohman went on.

"The crowded space was dreadful—the stench of vomit and urine and bodies sweating with heat and fever. I wanted to die—I thought I would, Perry.

One in five men would not survive. We tossed their corpses over the side each morning. If we were alone for a minute, we would haul buckets of seawater up and sluice them over our own filthy bodies before we were summoned into the horrid darkness below once more.

Just when I knew I could not take another day of this—we sighted port here in Haiti.

We were housed in a giant warehouse awaiting our new masters, grateful to be out in fresh air and sun and feel the rain on our faces. The Middle Passage was over at last."

"So when Bunt paid for you and you joined us, will that mean you won't be a slave anymore?" said Henry.

"Yeah! You can be a pirate—like us!" said Perry.

"I can only wonder how two skinny white boys ended up on a ship full of nasty buccaneers, but I assume you are as much a slave as I am—for the moment." Ohman grinned, showing his marvelous snow-white teeth and--by his words--his compassion for his fellow captives.

"Land ho!" hollered Birdy from the foretop.

Mad Dog shouted with glee: "Jamaica, boys! Rum and women and no fightin'!"

The whole crew was quivering with anticipation as their ship came round the south coast of Jamaica to the British town of Port Royal.

Perry and Henry were well aware of the legendary lair of Captain Henry Morgan—this was a town made famous by pirates!

"Well, Henry," said Perry. "We're pirates now, I wonder what homecoming will be like?"

For Ohman, it was bittersweet.

The boys soon learned that he was sold to a plantation owner for £33, 6 shillings—the going rate for African slaves.

Captain Dean said that--in today's money—they could multiply that by 50, which would make it about $2700 US. The price of a man's life in 1691.

As Ohman was carried in chains to the dock and the waiting carriage, he turned to the boys and gave that dazzling smile. The boys waved mournfully.

"God be with you!" shouted Perry. Then he wept.

Chapter Ten   Port Royal

On the balmy south coast of the island of Jamaica lay the British harbor known as Port Royal--seized from the Spanish in 1655 and fortified at its entrance.

Under the protection of the Royal Navy, a town sprang up and flourished on a spit of land protruding into the bay which became the legendary home for all buccaneers on the Spanish Main.

A town of 22,000 souls by 1660, it was from here that pirates such as Morgan and Calico Jack Rackham set out to raid the rich galleons bringing gold and silver from South and Central America to Spain.

Once they had dropped anchor in the bay, the crews of every vessel would row ashore, singing lustily in anticipation of enjoying all those things that men at sea are deprived of—strong drink, women, decently prepared food, and beds on floors that do not sway or heave with the swell of the ocean.

There was a ranking of authority--a pecking order as chicken farmers say—of *who* moored their ship *where* in the harbor.

As buccaneers and vessels with royal Letters of Marque grew bolder under the Jamaican governor

Edward D'Oley. Port Royal was now officially protected by The 'Brethren of the Coast'—a euphemism for 'pirates'.

Ironically, Britain seized Jamaica from the Spanish yet now allowed pirates to protect the island—although the British Royal Navy was the supreme maritime force in the Atlantic, Pacific, and Indian Oceans. His Majesty would employ that power to good use elsewhere—such as the East Indies and the Indian subcontinent where British dominance was becoming supreme.

Captain Wm. Bonney, Esq. and his entire 'staff' were therefore not only allowed a berth in what later became Kingston Bay, but they were welcomed--and took but little time to row ashore in their jolly boats, pulling them up on the sand, and tramping higgledy-piggledy into a port whose 'downtown' had swelled to seven-and-a-half thousand living in civilized dwellings that had sprung up of late on this shoreline of sunny Jamaica.

As the locals would say in their patois: "When jackass smell corn, him gallop."

So men of every race and personality flooded the streets and taverns and brothels of Port Royal like the tides of the sea—washing in, ebbing out—making

Port Royal not only the largest city in the Caribbean, but also a lucrative port of call for traders and merchants whose commerce spanned the globe.

Into this jostling crowd of seamen moved two boys from America—that future nation of Liberty— looking for a meal and a bed, since women and booze were not of much interest at their tender age.

The warehouses lined the actual harbor, while the streets led into the town where it was said that there existed one tavern for every ten residents.

Taverns were not only drinking places, but served meals and offered rooms upstairs for men with plenty of silver and gold to go round!

"How much shore leave are we supposed to have?" said Henry.

"There must be a signal among the men belonging to a particular ship that tells them when to go aboard again," said Perry.

"Let's keep an eye on our crew so we don't get completely swallowed up in this zoo of a port town. This is not at all like Fort Lauderdale," said Henry.

They knew from their reading that ships and navies of every nation often forcibly took boys as young as ten aboard to learn the ropes—literally.

It takes years to make a seasoned mariner so many well-known captains like James Cook or George Vancouver got their start in His Majesty's navy.

Boys from every town and village in England could find themselves invited—or forced by the press gang—to take to sea for months and years at a time.

"We could join the Navy, Perry," offered Henry. "Then we wouldn't have to be pirates for the rest of...I mean...while we are enjoying our holiday on the Atlantic."

"Think about it, Henry," Perry replied. "Do you really think the conditions and food are better on a navy ship? We would be at the bottom of the ladder in rank.

At least, on a pirate ship, we can leave any time we want. We have no indentured contract, no time to serve and toil with virtually no pay. We are free as any pirate!"

"Theoretically," said Henry.

"If we really wanted to find out, we could find some guys our age on shore leave, and ask them— swap stories of the sea and so on," continued Perry.

"That's not a bad idea. But where do we find them?"

"Look for anybody under five feet two," said Perry.

"Did you remember to bring some money?" asked Henry.

"I brought the pouch of coins I was given by the Quartermaster. Did you forget yours?"

"I think I did," said Henry with alarm.

"Is this it?" said Perry, dangling a small leather pouch with the initials H.S. in ink on it.

"Oh, thank God you brought it. If I lost it,…"

"Better keep that pen hidden, Henry. That ballpoint technology won't be invented for three hundred years and it would be awkward to explain to someone how you came to have it."

"I never thought of that. Even our clothing is odd enough to draw an occasional stare from someone," said Henry.

"Strangers in a strange land, my boy," said Perry, clapping Henry on the back.

"Let's spend some of this gold on food, shall we?"

***

Aside from bars, food was cooked fresh and served right on the street by local fishermen and their families.

"Come, boys, try dis." An older lady shoved a slab of board at them. "Dis one I catch and him cook myself."

The fish was steaming under shreds of ginger, cilantro and onion--with some kind of hot sauce. It came with flat bread on the side and a roasted yam so sweet it was like candy.

Twin wolves could not have consumed the meal faster!

"You be lookin' for a place to sleep tonight? My kids show you my house. I got clean beds with real cotton sheet," she explained.

"You pay me Spanish *reals*, I change you back wid English shillings. Dat be hokay?"

Henry and Perry nodded. That solves the next problem, Perry was thinking.

A skinny girl of about eight led them through an alleyway with balconies hung with laundry to dry and then up narrow steps to a solid three-storey dwelling which smelled of cooking.

Shy faces of young children peered as they climbed.

"Hi!" said Perry—to be greeted with giggles and smiles. Most of the children were clothed in homespun breeches and something like tank tops, and went shoeless even in the street.

The girl smiled and pointed to the wooden bucket near the door, seemingly reading Henry's mind.

She closed the door respectfully and her light footsteps could be heard going down until she met the other children whereupon she bawled out orders like she was the captain of the house.

"So far so good, Henry."

"We've got food and a bed. Now I want a hot shower."

"Keep dreaming, Henry. I noticed a cistern of water and a stone sink coming in. So at least we will get some kind of wash before breakfast."

"Just think, Perry. If we were older like Capt. Dean, we would be chugging ale and rum in some bar right now, and likely pass out on the floor. Not my idea of a good time."

"That's what frat life is like in college, Henry. We have something to look forward to!"

Henry laughed then yawned and slumped onto the mattress and remembered nothing until one very loud rooster woke them up sometime after sunrise.

***

The mistress of the house cooked for them—the same as she cooked for her brood of children—*burgoo* she called it, the same morning meal that most men at sea ate.

It was fundamentally cooked oatmeal with a variety of ingredients that were at hand. Mariners liked pork fat or bacon strips, Jamaicans like it with a dollop of molasses.

Some sliced melon, more fresh bread—the boys left the hostel feeling full and content.

By mid-morning the temperature was in the '80s and so was the humidity. Despite a cool wash earlier, Henry felt uncomfortable and shrugged off his shirt and tied it around his waist. The sun on his body felt good.

"I liked your idea of finding other boys our age to hang out with," he said to Perry.

"But where to find them? Where would *we* go during shore leave?" said Perry.

"I don't know…just wander around, I guess. Follow the grown-ups." Henry squinted as the sun rose higher and hotter. "Wish they had a swimming pool!"

"Hey! That's not a bad thought, Henry. Maybe the boys are down at the harbor having a dip."

Sure enough! There was a small quay with steps leading down to a patch of sandy beach and there were several boys jumping into the water and yelling like crazy.

"Hey!" one shouted. "Come join us!"

"I'm Herman," the tall boy said, "…and that's Melville," pointing at a slender lad splashing in the shallows.

They were about sixteen, Perry guessed, and quite muscular from the hard work that was given to every man and boy, regardless of age.

"We shipped out of Marseilles on a French *barque*," Herman continued. "Been at sea near six months now."

He looked at Perry and Henry—who, for the moment—were a bit shy about saying who they sailed with.

"Ah, we are on a nice ship with some pretty decent guys," Perry began. "Just stopped by Port Royal to pick up some supplies."

Henry made a circle in the sand with his toe, but said nothing.

"Right. You smell, mate. Come jump in the water and give yourself a wash," said Herman, waving at Melville.

Perry and Henry stripped down and waded into the remarkably warm seawater and got dunked right away.

"This feels great!" shouted Perry. Henry agreed.

"What do you guys do all day?" said Perry inquisitively.

It was Melville's turn to speak.

"We are supposed to be shadowing the First Mate but honestly—he's in his cups at the tavern all day."

"Yeah! And in the pants of some girl all night," said Herman.

"When does your ship sail?" asked Henry.

"We are in port for a fortnight," said Melville—who was obviously English.

"Long as they pay us enough to have food and a bed, we don't really care," admitted Herman.

"'sides," said Melville, "there's many men about who carelessly throw their money away, and some of us—not saying *us* in particular—spend the time picking pockets, which is easy if a man is passed out on the side of the road or draped over a barrel."

"Now take them pirates," he said. "They get their loot the easy way—holding up and raiding a fat merchantman or galleon. T'ain't fair!"

"Aye," said Herman. "T'ain't fair. We work our asses off for a handful of coins but pirates get sacks of gold. Am I right, Perry?"

Perry didn't know what to say for a moment.

"I'm sure a pirate's life must be…ah…rewarding—just as you say, Herman."

Henry was biting his nails as an excuse not to open his mouth. He knew Perry was a fast talker and would say the right thing.

"What say we go into town and see what's what," said Herman. "Grab some lunch there."

The very word 'lunch' was enticing to Henry in particular. He hadn't dared to think about The Malt Shop, and their friends all eating the delicious fries and burgers it was famous for.

But hunger is a boy's constant companion, so they quickly tightened their belts and laced their shoes and followed the older boys as they wended their way down a backstreet with surprising familiarity.

Even at this time of day, young women were calling out to them, their hair pinned and glossy with coconut oil, their lips stained crimson.

"Have you been with a girl before?" said Melville, looking at Perry and Henry with amusement on his face.

"Not lately," said Perry drily.

"The girls here know what it takes to please a man," said Melville with that certainty that only experience brings.

"I guess there's lots of ways to spend your money here," Perry replied.

"Aye," said Herman. "Lots."

They entered a smoky tavern that had an outdoor patio under an awning and sat down. The sign identified it as the *Moby Dick*.

Next to them was a table of men intensely involved in some card game like poker. Occasional curses or laughs would emerge as winners and losers declared themselves.

To Henry's lasting delight, Caribbean patties on bread were really quite close to being a burger— especially with tomato and something resembling relish added on top of the meat, green cilantro and spinach peeking out from the bun.

He ordered two—just in case his next meal was not as easy to obtain.

Perry had fried rice with shrimps, and steamed cassava root on the side. He declined the offer of rum and asked for beer—he later said to Henry: "You can't drink the water and they don't have Coke."

The older boys ate heartily as well, and for a moment it was a perfect world.

The gamblers were howling with rage and drink but the waiter knew this was just another normal day in Port Royal.

He leaned in toward the boys and said: "Every day de bucket go in de well, one day bottom mus' drop out!" and winked, as he retreated inside to fetch more food and rum, leaving the boys to contemplate the wisdom of what had been said.

The sun had now taken on a brassy hue and the humid air was stifling.

Without warning, the ground began to softly rock—not enough to scare anyone but it did topple some bottles inside the bar and Henry gave a look to Perry that showed he was concerned.

Saying goodbye to the others, Henry said: "That was a seismic tremor, Perry. That was a two-point-oh earthquake!"

"You think something bigger may come along?" said Perry.

"I have no idea about the geological history of Jamaica—or the Caribbean in general. But a quake of even moderate size could produce a *tsunami* that would make a real mess of any coastal town like Port Royal."

"Well, let's hope it happens when we are far away at sea," replied Perry.

"Which reminds me. How do we know when to go back to the ship? We'd better find somebody we know from *The Dragon's Breath* and get back in the loop," he stated.

As it turned out, the boys need not have worried. Their shipmates found them instead.

Chapter Eleven Stocking Up

"Now where have you two rascals got to?" said Postage. "We've got errands aplenty and only two arms apiece!"

"Sorry," said Perry. "We got lost."

"Lost indeed," said Handling, passing two large backpacks to each of the boys.

"Let's stock up, mon. Heaven knows how long we be at sea dis time!"

Postage and Handling had acquired their names from British merchants who had first given them work in this very port.

They had disappeared from the brutal sugar cane plantation inland in the Blue Mountains during a storm and—being strong and willing—they shipped aboard a British sloop that turned out to be manned by privateers. Being island folk, they were naïve and unaware of how the pirate trade actually worked.

Their ship was blown out of the water by a French man o'war near Martinique and they were taken to a slave market where the French traded them for local rum.

Everything has its price.

Later, they were sold to a certain Capt. Bonney who himself was sailing under a black flag.

"Pick it op, boys," said Postage. "Let's start wid de basics—root vegetables, sugar, and rice."

Anyone who has picked up a bag of rice knows that it can be quite heavy. Anyway, that's what Henry was thinking as they loaded a good forty pounds of it on his back. It was local grown and a fragrant variety that had originally come from India, and was called 'baz-matee'.

"Let's look t' de meat," said Handling, expecting Henry to just trot along like a puppy beside him.

Henry staggered once or twice but soon adapted his pace to the load.

"What about fruit?" asked Perry.

"We've no need for dat," said Postage. "Give you de runs."

"Well, what about Vitamin C?" he said.

"What the hell is dat? N'er heered of it, mon." Both men were looking up from sacks and tables of foodstuffs.

"Ah, it's...a quality of fruit that can help prevent scurvy," said Perry finally.

"Oh, d'you know 'bout dat scurvy? Can you help de men get healed of dat?" Now Postage was definitely listening. He knew he could take the credit for bringing healthy foods onto the ship.

"Absolutely!" said Perry confidently.

"We'll choose the right fruit for our crew," added Henry. He slipped out of the heavy pack of rice and set it down.

"Citrus?" said Henry.

"You got it!" said Perry.

"Let's get whatever they have—limes, lemons, maybe oranges or tangerines if we are really lucky."

They stuffed ten pounds of fresh citrus fruit into Perry's backpack and hurried to catch up with Postage and Handling who were haggling over a pork barrel with a nasty looking merchant who had a nasty looking machete blade protruding from his belt.

"You be no better dan a tief!" the merchant was saying.

Perry interjected before things got any worse.

"We pay in gold," he said, leveling his gaze at the man's eyes, whose expression immediately softened.

"Oh, dat be de case, we can do bizness," he smiled.

Perry slipped a doubloon from his pocket and waved it under the merchant's nose.

Postage and Handling just stood stock still—not quite believing that a cabin boy was proving that he was a man after all, by standing up to this merchant.

"Fill it," said Perry, taking Handling's leather pouch and thrusting it toward the container of pork.

Suddenly, Handling came to life and said, "Lemme have a smell," and nodding his approval, they took more than half a barrel—probably a good fifty pounds.

The merchant grinned and the gap where his bottom teeth should have been spoiled his smile, but he snatched the gold piece from Perry's fingers like a heron spears a fish.

"You did good on dat one," said Postage approvingly as they lugged the food down to one of the rowboats, and thence to the ship.

"Where are the other men? Where is the captain?" Perry asked.

"Dunno. Try de King's Head tavern. All de captains go to dat one. Too pricey for de likes of us sailors," said Postage.

***

They found the captain alright—and he was sober and in a relatively good mood.

"There you are," said Capt. Bonney as if he had just been looking for them.

"What do you need us to do, Captain?" said Perry.

"I need more crew," he said. "And I need a ship's doctor. Find me one of those, if you truly want to help."

"We will do our best, sir," said Perry doubtfully.

"Are men deserting our ship?" asked Henry as they went out to the street once more.

"Don't ask me," said Perry. "I suppose if there were an alternative, some might be tempted. I could see where a man might choose to live on shore and buy some land and start a family, instead of the rough and treacherous life of a buccaneer."

"What choice do *we* have?" lamented Henry. "Are we doomed to sail The Seven Seas like the ghost ship

The Flying Dutchman? Never to see home and family again? Trapped in time?

Now I understand how emotional it must have been for you, Perry, when you had your time-slips!" Henry said.

"Yes," said Perry. "I was at the mercy of the Fates and yet I never lost hope."

He turned and seized Henry by both shoulders.

"Nor can *we*, Henry Schuyler! Like your brave ancestor in the struggle for America's independence", we must soldier on—believing that we make a difference because we stand for what is right!"

Perry surprised his friend with his passionate outburst.

But Perry went on.

"We will not be pirates forever. Something will happen. We come from the land of Life, Liberty & The Pursuit of Happiness, and somehow—some way—we will go, yet leave a little light along the path we tread!"

"I'm glad it's us, Perry. Just the two of us. We are friends forever and that won't change," said Henry.

" See: *The Ghost of Lantern Bridge* Book 5 in the series

"But can you forgive me for getting you into this mess in the first place, Henry?"

"I came because I wanted to. I came because I want to experience more of life than just an ordinary boy living in an ordinary town could ever do.

Since I met you, a whole new world of astonishing and amazing things has opened to me.

If we ever get back to Brackendale, I am going to have a hard time sitting in a classroom or doing homework or cutting the grass.

Can you understand me, Perry? Come what may, our lives are destined to be charmed—or cursed-- depending on how you look at it.

Either way, I'm going down that road—and you're going with me. That's enough for me, Perry."

"I guess we'd better go find a doctor for the captain, and somehow convince him (or her) that providing medical attention to a crew of pirates is an attractive career choice!" said Perry.

He wiped the sweat of another hot Jamaican afternoon from his forehead with a rag, and they disappeared into yet another darkened tavern where the air temperature was five degrees lower and a cold beer could quench the nagging thirst and wash the dust of the town from a man's mouth.

To their surprise, a familiar face greeted them and they sat down with a pint to speak with him.

"Capt. Dean! It's so good to see you!" said Henry.

"Likewise Henry," said the captain of the former *Mary Celeste*. "Perry—you look older with your hair longer and a tan that would make a Hollywood star envious."

Perry laughed.

"And you don't look a day over forty, Capt. Dean," said Perry. "I am still racking my brains for a scientific explanation of how time travel has made you a younger man.

But you look great! Wait till your cronies in Florida see you! They won't recognize you!" Perry said enthusiastically.

Thom Dean drained his glass and pointed to it so that the server could bring a refill.

"Well Perry—that's the thing. I've come to a decision.

I don't see any point in returning to the States, to my old miserable life just sitting on a bench from morning to night, dreaming of better days.

I have nothing to return to you see.

But here—here I have *adventure*. I have new experiences that have given me pleasure.

All I've ever wanted is to work on a ship, be a part of that marvelous tradition of seamanship, smell the salt air and feel the wind on my face.
I don't need to know why going through that portal--or whatever you want to call it—made me youthful again.
And I am not giving that up.

What I'm saying, boys, is that this is where I stay. 'Living the dream' my old Dad used to say."

"I think I understand," said Henry. "Life is where you can *live* it best, and your 'best' is right here in 1691."
Henry reached over and shook Capt. Dean's weathered hand.

"Any idea where we can find a doctor for Capt. Bonney?" said Perry, after a hearty handshake with Thom Dean—their old friend.

"As a matter of fact, I met a Scotsman named D. R. Stuart only this morning. He expressed a wish to go to sea. Let me see if I can spot him."
Thom got to his feet and surveyed the room.

"There! That's the man. Go ask him what his availability is. I'm not sure he would want to know that you are pirates, though.
"Good luck, boys, and God bless!"

Perry and Henry left Thom Dean sitting at a table with a cold pint of ale in his hand, happy and contented with a second chance at Life.

"Excuse me...Doctor Stuart?" asked Perry.

"Aye. That'll be me." He was a clean-shaven, decently attired man of about fifty.

"We have orders from our captain to find a physician to serve on our ship, sir. I cannot speak to the wages, but our captain is an honorable man and our crew much in need of a surgeon...you know, who can stitch up wounds and gashes and deal with…ah…such things."

Perry and Henry tried to minimize the true nature of their vessel and its crew.

"So ye are pirates then, is that what you're saying, laddie?"

"*Nice* pirates, sir," replied Perry with a hopeful smile.

"Yeah, we've never killed anyone or raped and pillaged, or anything…" added Henry.

"You both look like you belong at home with your family, milking cows or digging potatoes," replied Dr. Stuart.

"That would be kind of nice about now," muttered Henry.

"Show me your captain, then. Maybe we can strike a bargain." Dr. Stuart finished his pint and stood up and followed the boys to where they had left Capt. Bonney.

They passed *The Moby Dick.*
"Weird name for a restaurant," said Henry.
"Wasn't the name of the white whale in that book?"

"*That book* was published in 1851," Perry said. "What's weird is that a bar in Jamaica in 1691 has the same name."

Perry brought the older gentleman inside. "Capt. Bonney, sir—meet Dr. Duncan Stuart."

"Ahh, good doctor. A Scotsman I believe."

"Aye. Trained in Edinburgh. Got shanghaied to come down to this wretched island with the Navy and I'm still looking for a way to get off," said the doctor.

"Perhaps I can help," said Bonney ordering a round of ale.

"We are a small crew of about twenty, but are afflicted with the usual maladies that go with seafaring. Stomach upset, bone and joint injuries, cuts and scrapes—that sort of thing."

"You wouldn't also have men with syphilis? Or grave wounds from grapeshot and musket fire? Or scurvy?"

"You are a man after my own heart," said Bonney. "You've discerned all our ailments in the time it takes to drain a draught of ale."

"I will pay you in gold, and in return—you will obey every command I give, including—but not limited to—amputation. Are we in agreement on this, Dr. Stuart?"

"Aye, sir. I'll fetch my tools and await your instructions. Perhaps your young assistants here will help me find my way aboard."

Capt. Bonney looked at Perry, who nodded in assent.

"Cheers, good Doctor Stuart," said Capt. Bonney. "You've made it easy for me," Bonney said. "The last surgeon we had I had to enlist on pain of death.

We sail in three days. My vessel has a dragon bowsprit and flies a black flag."

"Many fly that flag, Captain," said Stuart. "I'll be depending on your lads here."

Dr. Stuart took his leave.

Capt. Bonney gave that look of "Well done, boys!" to Perry and Henry. "The Bos'un's got a bead on some fresh recruits," he said.

"You were helping Postage and Handling with the food, am I right?"

"How did you know, sir?" asked Perry.

"I have eyes and ears, boys. Stupid captains don't remain captains very long.

Now go find those two and see what they've got up to. Tell 'em we sail on Saturday—at dawn!"

"Aye, sir," said Henry and Perry simultaneously.

It was near to suppertime so the boys went back to the restaurant they had brunch in—perhaps hoping to have a last word with Herman and Melville—but the patio was empty except for a stray cat sunning herself in a corner. And about ten thousand flies—some of which were the biting kind.

***

The island had onshore winds in the morning called 'the doctor's wind', and winds that blew from the land to the sea in the evening called 'the undertaker's wind'. The latter made the day's heat dissipate and made it much more comfortable to be out after 6 pm.

One area of market that they had not explored was the Chinese market—which had its own little corner of the town.

On a whim, Perry and Henry asked for directions and soon found the charming district, festooned with red lanterns and paper dragons hung from rafters.

In one corner a lively conversation was going on—and to the boys' consternation—it was Postage and Handling right in the middle of it.

Wherever *they* went, there was commotion, Perry said to Henry.

"No way, no!" a Chinese merchant was shouting at the two black men standing at a table that was covered in strings of pearls and bowls of loose pink pearls that glowed--even as the sun went down.

"You worse than pirate!" the Chinese continued.

Perry whispered to Henry: "They *are* pirates." Henry chuckled.

"Be cool now," said Postage. "We gonna give you a good price for dem white pearls. Looka—I show you how I gonna pay. Dis *gold*, real gold!"

He placed some doubloons on his palm as if to prove he had the cash.

"How 'bout we go into bizness?" said Handling.

"We gib you good price, fair price--den we sell dose in Cuba, come back here, buy more. Good plan?"

"I give you these ones," said the pearl merchant, lifting a couple of strands for them to see, but keeping a yard back in case they snatched and ran.

Those kind of things happen in markets like these.

"No, mon—dis not good quality. Look! Not even round--dis one. Not gonna fetch a good price. Gimme best ones and say your best price."

There was an understanding that haggling over price was part of the transaction, but there was a limit.

Postage fingered the gold coins in his hand and the Chinese watched them as they glinted in the dying light.

He turned to another couple of men behind him and had a brief exchange.

"Hokay! I give you best ones! I give you this..." and he extended his arm with two lovely strings of pearls as white as moonlight.

"And I give you *this*," he said threading some of the pink pearls on a thread with amazing speed and dexterity. These men were pros. Perry and Henry could see that.

Postage handed the man four coins of gold and three more of silver—and the deal was done.

Henry sighed with relief. He had spotted two men in the shadows with long curved blades in their belt sash—he was guessing they were a Chinese-style broadswords and that they were likely razor sharp.

No fight, no problem.

The Chinese was smiling and bowing, the two cooks were mimicking him and backing away into the street.

"Ah, hi," said Perry, startling both of them.

"What da hell, mon. You bin stalkin' us?"

"No, no. Captain Bonney said to go find you and tell you we sail on the weekend. Just following orders, guys!"

"Fine. *'Pig never know de use a dem tail so till butcher chop it off'*," said Handling and both men started to roar with laughter over a joke that just went over the heads of the boys.

They veered off to the lane that led them back to the hostel and climbing the stairs they noticed that the landlady had washed their clothing.

It was hanging on the rail and was almost dry.

The sheets were fresh, too.

Both boys tumbled into their beds and mumbled a few words to the ceiling and then were quiet.

The whole town was quiet tonight it seemed.

Even pirates have to sleep sober sometimes.

Chapter Twelve   A Wee Misadventure

It was on the way back into the center of the town that the trouble began.

Was it not enough that Port Royal was full of cutthroats, murderers and low-lifes of every sort? There were also thieves who would steal anything not nailed down.

That included lovely bright pearls—which Postage and Handling had just acquired at some cost from the Chinese pearl market.

So when the duo sat down for a well-deserved bite to eat, their satchels full of treasure were being carefully removed from under their chair by two youthful lads--with sticky fingers.

And the pirates would have lost everything except that Henry and Perry just happened to see the whole thing happen from the next table where they were sitting.

"Stop! Thief!" shouted Henry.

"Fire!" said Perry. That got everyone's attention.

All heads turned and the thieves retreated to the alley.

But that wasn't the end of it!

In came four burly men accompanied by the would-be thieves and strode up to the table.

"Yer late, boys," said a man so large his head banged the overhead lamp.

"Come along nice, now, or we'll have to use a bit of force," said another huge fellow with a gold hoop of enormous size dangling from each earlobe.

The twin cooks were in no mood to leave their evening meal behind at the request of a thug.

"Late for what?" said Perry as they hustled him out of the café.

"We sail at midnight, and you'll be aboard right snappy, boy!" said the man with the earrings.

"I think you've made a mistake," continued Perry in a wavering voice. "We belong to another ship, I can assure you."

"The only mistake is resistin', I can assure *you*!" said the big man pulling and dragging the hapless pirates down the alley toward the docks.

"Throw 'em in the boat," said their leader.

The sky in the west was a faint purple when the four members of *The Dragon's Breath* crew were ferried out to a two-masted ship flying a Union Jack.

They spent the night on the main deck, curled up like possums and flinching from mosquito bites on every exposed bit of flesh.

***

In the morning, they were served burgoo along with the regular crew, and then the captain addressed them.

"We welcome you aboard the *Jamestown*. We are short of a full complement of men—so we invited you on board to help us sell our shipment of tobacco in our scheduled ports-of-call.

The we return to Virginia and load up again."

He looked at Perry and Henry.

"You'll be treated fair and paid your due. Your companions..." he nodded in the direction of the two black cooks, "...will be sold once we reach the colony."

Postage and Handling could only groan and weep at the cruelty of their fate—escaped slaves in Jamaica now doomed to be slaves in Virginia or Carolina.

Perry spoke up boldly and perhaps rashly in defense of the two black men.

"You have no right to take these men against their will and sell them into slavery!" he fairly shouted.

"They are free men whose skin color happens to be dark but which does not condemn them to servitude by those of a lighter tone!"

"Well, well. You speak like the men in the Legislative Assembly," said the captain. "They call for emancipation of the Africans—especially our liberal cousins up in Massachusetts!"

Perry was stunned for a moment? *Massachusetts?*

That is in the United States! This is an American ship—before there was an America!

He looked at Henry with that look that told Henry a big surprise was coming for this young captain.

Perry leapt to his feet. To everyone's surprise he loosened his belt and opened his Levis to reveal an American flag sewn into the lining.

"See this flag?" he shouted. "This is the flag of a great nation being born--born in Virginia and Georgia, born in Carolina and Massachusetts and New York!"

"I have come from the Future, from the United States of America, to bring you news—and a warning!"

By now, every man and boy was sitting cross-legged on the deck staring raptly at Perry Normal from Brackendale, New York.

The captain was nervously stoking and smoking his long clay pipe--but didn't say one word!

"I tell you that these Thirteen Colonies of His Majesty will one day throw off the yoke of Tyranny and birth a nation like none ever seen before."

Perry mounted the quarterdeck and leaned into the rail facing the main deck and mainmast.

"A new nation, conceived in Liberty and dedicated to the proposition that all men are created equal," Perry continued.

"What has transpired at Jamestown and Roanoke, is being repeated at Boston, and New York, and Baltimore. At Savannah and Philadelphia.

Men greater than ourselves will build it, and defend its principles of Liberty and Equality. We are the forerunners, gentlemen! We are the vanguard of Democracy!"

Perry pounded with his fist on the mahogany rail with each phrase. Much like Patrick Henry would do in the Virginia legislature less than one hundred years later.

The captain's mouth hung open; the bosun was scratching his head muttering a word he had never before heard—'Democracy...democracy?'.

The First Mate called out: "Well, what's the warning, sir?"

Henry noted the respect in his use of the word 'sir'.

"The warning is that slavery is going to be seen as evil, as a wrong against persons of color—and if it is allowed to flourish, a terrible war will tear this magnificent experiment in democracy to shreds!

We can stop it—if we begin now, before its dark roots take permanent hold in the Colonies.

Have no part in it, Captain," Perry said, glaring right at the man.

"My friend and I must return to the land from whence we came, so heed what we say!"

With that, Perry stepped down and all the men on deck parted like the Red Sea for Moses as he stepped toward the stern rail—motioning for Henry to rise and follow.

"Fare thee well, Captain of the *Jamestown*!" Perry said, as he pulled on one of the sheets to lift himself up on the gunwale and--together with his dear friend Henry—hurled himself from that height into the blue waters of the bay.

The two boys swam almost leisurely toward the dockside; no one fired a gun, no one yelled.

Even as they swung up onto the timbers and the decking at dockside, nary a word from the *Jamestown* would be heard across the water.

Men on that ship would later whisper that these were witches or sorcerers in disguise--something demonic that was best left alone!

Not long after—by midmorning—the two-master lifted anchor and was not seen in Port Royal again.

PART III   SHIVER ME TIMBERS

CHAPTER THIRTEEN   I SEE STARS

Saturday came and most of the men on *The Dragon's Breath* were accounted for—most.

Among the missing were Postage and Handling and the carpenter Jim Beam.

Also missing were the two Chinese pearl merchants Ming and Tian; Perry could not say whether he saw them at the pearl market the day Postage and Handling went missing or not.

On the other hand, there were two Frenchmen who had defected from a Spanish ship, and a new ship's doctor from Scotland who was dressed as nicely as any doctor in his practice room in Europe.

Given the chaos that characterized this wild Jamaican seaport, it is not surprising that men go missing.

What *is* surprising is that many do make it back to their ship—some hung-over, some limping or in bandages—but they straggle back, ready for more maritime adventures of the pirate kind!

The breeze was steady as the ship made a course for Cuba as the wealthy merchant ships and cargo vessels all had to exit the Caribbean by sailing due east—passing Cuba and Florida, past Hispaniola and Puerto Rico and the Bahamas—until the open ocean lay glittering before them.

Men since the time of Columbus had learned the secrets of the tradewinds and currents that made crossing to Africa and Europe almost a routine matter.

Mad Dog McGuinty was complaining that he had lost all his money in port. Everyone knew that 'lost' meant you spent it all recklessly and heedlessly.

Mad Dog was not the only one who was broke; that applied to 99% of every man aboard—even the Captain who appeared on the quarterdeck wearing some fine new clothing and black patent leather shoes with brass buckles!

"I don't smell it yet," said Mad Dog.

"Smell what?" asked Perry.

"A victim, lad. A prize! I can smell 'em on the wind like as a wolf smells a sheep beyond the hill."

"Wishful thinking, Henry," said Perry to Henry.

"Who knows what sailors' noses tell them?" said Henry. "I know they can 'read' the wind and the tides, and tell you what the weather will be three days ahead."

"Can I tell you something, Henry?"

"Shoot!"

"I think Capt. Bonney is not such a great navigator, and that's why he hired McComb to pilot the ship," said Perry.

"Where are you going with this?" Henry replied.

"I think that nobody—including McComb—is using latitude or longitude to determine our location, let alone plot a course.

Their maps are also wrong—just approximations of *what* is *where*. That is why it impressed the hell out of the captain when I sketched the whole Caribbean basin for him not long after we were captured. Remember?

And this problem is compounded by the rivalry between Spain, Portugal, Holland, France and England.

Everybody has their own cartographers and therefore their preferred maps—all of which are jealously guarded.

So it's like we are sailing around the ocean blindfolded."

"You have an idea, don't you Perry!"

"Let's use what we 21st century scholars know about geography to improve the navigational skills of our crewmates, Henry."

"Using basic Math, right?"

"That's why I brought you along, Henry!" Perry said playfully. "You're the Math geek!"

"Well, latitude is a simple geometric calculation really. Determine the angle between the North Star Polaris and the horizon. The angular measure in degrees is equivalent to our latitude on Planet Earth."

"Good boy, Henry. So if we can figure that measurement out, we will know how close to—or far from—the Equator we are.

For example, Brackendale New York is about 43 degrees North Latitude, give or take."

"I'm guessing we are less than twenty degrees North right now," said Henry.

"Let's wait till the stars come out, and we will test your estimation, my boy."

"But longitude is a whole other thing, Perry!"

"It will be very difficult to do because there is one piece of equipment that we absolutely *must have*—a reliable timepiece. A chronometer. A clock, Henry!"

"Umm, that is because we need to know with precision what the time in London, England is. That is where the Prime Meridian—zero degrees of Longitude—is situated. And every line of longitude—east or west of Greenwich England—is calculated in relation to that Prime Meridian."

"Dead on, Henry! In 1691—where we happen to be stuck at the moment—no one knew any of this, although sailors and travelers had been trying to construct a grid system on maps to make location easier," said Perry.

"If I had my cell with me—it has GPS."

"No, Henry. No satellites in near-Earth orbit for another 276 years!"

"Oh, right. I forgot. It is so frustrating trying to function in a world without electronics."

"When we get you back home, Henry, we'll go shopping for some new toys!" Perry said.

"*If* we get back home, Perry. That's a big *IF.*"

Perry confounded the crew by setting up a primitive sundial to determine 'solar noon'—a preliminary measurement to find longitude.

"The shadow is shortest at noon," Perry explained to Quartermaster Bunt, who was nosing about.

If you weren't priming cannon or swabbing the decks, Bunt would give you the evil eye--like the Math teacher Kruschevsky at Brackendale when he saw you were slacking off in class.

"What we need, Quartermaster Bunt, is a timepiece. You don't happen to have one in your pocket do you?"

Bunt snorted sarcastically.

"Aye, sure—I carry one wherever I go so I won't be late," he said.

"I'm serious," said Perry. "If we can determine the time in London and guess the time *here*—which will be about five hours later—we can make a decent guess at our longitude, and therefore our precise location."

"I didn't have the benefit of an education like you boys," he said. "But I will find you what you need.

Wait here," and Bunt slipped down the hatchway to below decks—leaving Henry and Perry wondering what he was going to do.

They didn't have to wait long.

"Will this do?" said Bunt.

He held out a shining pocket watch with metal case and cover and inside an elegant watch face with antique hands and winding stem.

"Wow! This is awesome, sir. How did you--?"

"It's the captain's. He agreed to loan it for now on account of your little experiment. For gawd's sake, don't drop it overboard or something. The captain will throw me in after it!"

"It reads 7 o'clock, Henry, which I take to be the morning in London, since it is just past midday here."

"And the Earth rotates 15° every 60 minutes. So 15 * 5.25 = 78.75° West Longitude here at Port Royal," said Henry.

"That lines up almost exactly with New York City and Washington, D.C.," exclaimed Perry.

"Now I feel better," Henry said. "It's like we're kind of close to home--you know, Perry?"

"Thank you, Mr. Bunt," said Perry returning the watch to the large rough hand of the seaman.

"Once night falls, we will take measurements and get our latitude," Perry said to Henry.

"Let's figure out how we're going to do it," said Henry, and the two boys trotted off like they were on a school field trip--instead of somewhere lost at sea with a gang of bloodthirsty pirates!

In the tropics, the sun sinks rapidly, and the night comes on swiftly.

The first thing that was apparent to the two young adventurers is that—without light pollution from large cities and towns—the stars seemed to be alive and pulsating, rather than shining and twinkling in the dark vault overhead.

They had no trouble discerning Polaris—not far from the handle of The Big Dipper (or Ursa Major their astronomer friends in Rochester preferred to call it).

Last year Perry had made some interesting findings using the telescopes at the university observatory—which led Perry to Pasadena and NASA JPL headquarters for a brief internship*.

"Here's what we do, Perry," said Henry.

"I've made a crude protractor out of a piece of bark. We use the horizon as a baseline, and angle another stick right at the star and measure the interior angle between the two."

"Okay. I'll hold the two sticks and you do the angular measurement, Henry. Boy, does this remind me of school!"

"Ahhh...hold it steady...eighteen! It is an 18° angle from the horizon to the North Star. That means that we are standing...ah...floating at eighteen degrees North Latitude."

"Perfect, Henry! We have a fix on our location that's as good as any geo-location device. We have proved that simple calculations can tell our captain with a high degree of certainty, wherever we are at any given point in time!"

"Just one thing, Perry!" Henry said.

· see: Perry Normal & The Moons of Saturn

"What's that, Henry?"

"We *have to* remind Capt. Bonney to wind his watch! If that watch stops, we cannot know London time, and cannot determine longitude. Which will be like walking with one leg in a cast!"

"We'll point that out to him when we deliver the exciting news—we are never going to be 'lost at sea' again!"

    ***

"Boys—come over here a minute, will ya?"

It was Quartermaster Bunt speaking—standing having a smoke with McComb and staring out at the pastel colors of the breaking dawn.

"Aye, sir," said the two.

"Look at yon vessel hove to just offshore."

They had journeyed by night to the northeast around the cape at Port Morant and left Jamaica behind, as they set a course for Santo Domingo—the town Columbus established for Spain in 1493.

The huge green mass of Hispaniola loomed ahead as the captain mulled what to do next.

"What flag d'ye see on yon mast. It's not pirate colors," said Bunt.

Perry's pulse jumped.

The flag was comprised of thirteen red and white stripes alternating horizontally, with a blue field in the upper left corner containing a circle of thirteen stars.

"I recognize the stripes, sure enough," said McComb. "That's the British East India Company...only—."

He paused, took his pipe out of his mouth and raised a spyglass to one eye.

"Only she's got some other symbols in the corner where the Union Jack should be. Sumpin' with stars."

"Let me see please," begged Perry.

Sure enough—there were white stars all in a circle on an indigo canton; not quite British, and not quite anything else--but what the boys knew to be 'Old Glory'.

"That's an American flag, sir!" Perry blurted out.

"American? What the devil is 'American'?" said Bunt.

"I mean, it's from the colonies in America—British colonial territory--so this vessel must have come from Virginia or Massachusetts, or something," Perry explained.

"I see ye've used yer time ashore to do some kind of spying, have ye? Have ye said ought to the captain?" said Bunt.

"No sir. But Henry and I did have a wee encounter with Virginian slavers back in Port Royal."

"They tried to shanghai us, sir!" shouted Henry.

Perry failed to mention that they had been caught 'spying' and narrowly escaped!

"Ye don't say," said Bunt. "But ye gave 'em the slip, didya?"

"So to speak, sir—yes!" said Perry, slyly winking at Henry, who was grinning at the memory of their leave-taking from the *Jamestown.*

"What they be carrying, McComb?" Bunt said to The Pilot.

"Likely slaves if they are inbound. Taking on sugar and trading for it with tobacco leaf—as I hear it grows well in Virginia," McComb said.

"Don't let McGuinty get a load of them. He's desperate for a prize and a pirate hungry for gold is a truly dangerous man!" said the quartermaster, who slipped below to notify the captain that Santo Domingo was close at hand.

"Creep up alongside, Quartermaster," said Bonney with the spyglass pressed to his face.

"Let's lower the Jolly Roger and raise an English flag on the staff. We don't want to announce ourselves as pirates—and thus alarm them.

We need information and they may be just the ones to give it to us!"

The black flag fell to the deck and just as quickly the Union Jack was raised and fluttered in the breeze.

"Quartermaster! Prepare a longboat. Arm yourselves discreetly. We are not boarding, we are chatting.

Take a small keg of that dandy rum we acquired in Port Royal. That should loosen their tongues," said Bonney with a chuckle.

Sure enough, once the longboat swept alongside the American merchantman, her men were hoisted aboard and Capt. Bonney could see a lively discussion had ensued. He knew the rum would grease the wheels of conversation.

"Is that the vessel that you saw in Port Royal?" said the captain to Perry.

"No, Captain. This is a bit larger and has three masts—built for trans-Atlantic trade I suppose."

"I haven't yet figured out where you boys hail from, but I will say one thing—you have an excellent overall knowledge of many things useful to me and to this ship.

Your little latitude/longitude lesson was most impressive. I don't think the men on this ship can match you.

That's one reason why I don't want to lose you. I can't replace you.

And I've grown fond of you. You're honest and can be relied on. Enough said."

The longboat returned by and by; whoever was rowing was doing a bad job, and uproarious laughter floated up as they pulled along the starboard side and clambered up to the main deck.

"That there was good rum," said Slash.

"Not like vodka—but drinkable," said Pistoff.

"What did you learn, my hearties?" said Capt. Bonney.

"As ye said, sir, she's a slaver bound for the Thirteen Colonies. Captain is an old salt and once he opened up, he gave us some news that is well worth our trouble."

"Say on, McGuinty!"

"They just came out of Santo Domingo and had overheard the crew of two Spanish vessels of war remark that they are to sail round the island in haste.

There is a massive shipment of gold and silver bullion and coins heading back to Sevilla in Spain.

The Governor of the island Francisco de Bobadilla let the news slip that King Philip IV kicked the bucket—probably in grief after his Austrian wife passed suddenly."

"Get to the point, McGuinty," said the captain, growing impatient.

"Aye, sir. As I was sayin', the new king—Charles II is rather--how shall we say? Impoverished.

As a result, as much Peruvian gold and Mexican silver as his fleet of galleons can carry are set to depart The New World as soon as the winds will permit."

McGuinty stopped to burp and wipe his mouth.

"That means they will be passing Cuba or Hispaniola in the next few days," said Capt. Bonney slowly.

"One of those ships *has our name on it*," he said.

To which McGuinty and most of the men cheered.

"You didn't by chance get a description, did you boys?" asked Capt. Bonney with a sly smile.

Captain Bonney was nearly as broke as his men, and besides—he was a pirate through and through.

With or without the consent of the British authority to act as a privateer—seizing and plundering all vessels at war with or in competition with British ships—he would not miss a chance to catch the immense treasure ships that passed south of Florida on their way to Spain.

"Sir," said McGuinty, now slumped on the gunwale between the oaken ribs of the ship, ready to pass out from the rum.

"Sir—the largest of them all is called *El Gordo*—The Fat One. Sir."

At that, McGuinty fell over in a dead sleep and the men just tossed a tarp over him and went below to eat.

CHAPTER FOURTEEN   WHAT ARE THE ODDS?

"Timing—everything is timing," Captain Bonney started the conversation in his private quarters after dinner.

"We need to cut them off just after they pass Cuba and are most vulnerable in open water," he continued.

"They'll be traveling as a convoy, sir," said Bunt.

"And with Spanish men-o'-wars with state-of-the-art cannon." The new ship's doctor Duncan Stuart added this detail that he himself had gleaned from the Americans.

"Well, we hit 'em the way we always do, gentlemen.

We board them quick as a snake, and take the captain and officers hostage.

Some of our men go below to survey and start to remove the treasure.

This is hard work so I recommend men like Ogultan—who can lift two of us in the air at the same time—and Pistoff, our Russian bear, take charge of this part of the operation.

Birdy and Perry and Henry will go aloft and cut rigging and sails—slashing rents and holes in everything they can reach."

Capt. Bonney paused to pour more wine.

"Speaking of slashing—Slash will be turned loose on the crewmembers who are unlucky enough to be at the pointed end of his sword.

Mad Dog will similarly earn his nickname--as he goes berserk with cutlass and pistol on deck.

My experience is that any captain with an ounce of intelligence will surrender fairly immediately once the deck gets slippery with his men's blood!"

"Why don't you seize her and drive her to land—then carry out your pillage and destruction?" said Stuart.

"Pirates don't work that way, good doctor Stuart," replied Bonney. "Too complicated. Unless we are severely damaged or un-navigable, we return to our own ship. The goal is to optimize the robbery part—and minimize the slaughtering part.

Pirates—at least some of us—don't enjoy murdering people. We are just trying to make a living here, men. Not get ourselves hanged."

"What about the ladies aboard the enemy vessel?" Stuart persisted in his questions; after all, he was new to being a pirate.

"Good question," said Bonney. "It can go either way. It is better to leave them screaming and fussing since that confuses the enemy and distracts them from the fact that their gold is disappearing over the side into our longboats."

Bonney continued. "On the other hand, suppose the treasure is pitifully small or not worth fighting and losing men over?

In that case, we grab—okay, that is a bit hostile—we 'assist' the pretty damsels and wives to disembark and accompany us to our ship, and then later we ransom them off for as much gold as we can."

"You've got it all planned out, sir!" said Dr. Stuart.

"That's why *I am the captain*," said Captain Bonney with a wide smile.

***

"Convoy in sight, Captain!" shouted Bunt, rushing to the quarterdeck to hand Capt. Bonney the spyglass.

"Prepare battle stations, men!" the captain shouted.

"Vot iss 'bettlestashuns?" said Pistoff. "Since venn we got zoes? Nobody tells me naw-sink!"

Perry and Henry helped get the cannon primed and loaded down below.

Each cannonball was muzzle-loaded--once the priming charge of gunpowder was placed at the breech end of the gun. Fuses were attached. Guns were rolled into their ports—ready to fire.

On deck, only the jibsail stayed up—the others were reefed to help them keep a low profile and blend in with the flat blues and greys of the water.

Muskets and pistols were primed and loaded, too. Perry and Henry each got one of each.

Slash had made sure that this time they also had serviceable blades—sharpened and wrapped with leather thongs on the handle, for better grip.

The boys knew this would be violent beyond anything they had ever experienced.

They knew in their hearts that once you kill a man, you can never 'unkill' him. It was a final act. It was not a game.

Perry swallowed hard as he thrust his pistol and knife into his belt.

A sharp cry came from the decks of *El Gordo*: 'Los bucaneros!' and at once torches were lit and men were scrambling in confusion.

Still, the guard ships had not noticed anything and that gave them a window of opportunity to board the massive galleon.

"Timing is everything," muttered Dr. Stuart as he clambered onto the rope ladder leading down to the boat rocking in the water.

The Dragon's Breath drew up on the port side in the lee of the wind and hidden from the cannon of the man o' war closest to *El Gordo*.

Slash and Ogultan took no boats: they swung out from the yardarms and landed plunk! Right on the deck!

The others slithered down the ladder and rowed to the bow section of the galleon and clambered up the side with grappling hooks and little tools that worked like ice picks that mountaineers use.

They were also sharp and deadly when they tore into a man's chest!

Perry had rushed to go over the side with Henry right behind.

"Owww," shouted Henry. "I've twisted my ankle, Perry." He was down with a leg in the air.

Perry turned at the railing but Henry waved him off.

"Go! Do your job! I'll be alright here. Nobody is going to attack *this* ship," he said.

Perry disappeared. Henry slid across the deck to rest against a mast--massaging his ankle.

Musket fire popped and lead balls whizzed through the smoke as lanterns toppled—setting fire to straw and coils of jute rope on their deck that had been oiled so it could slide through the pulleys easier.

Mad Dog was cursing in English and the enemy was cursing *en español*!

The biggest pirates vaulted down the hatch to the hold—where the treasures were kept.

The guardians of the treasure were not armed, so they played stupid.

"*Donde es el oro?*" shouted Bunt.

"No sé, Senõr," they replied.

Ogultan just busted through a wooden gate and pried open a floor covering, and started tossing bricks of pure gold onto the floor near Bunt and Pistoff, who started stuffing them in sturdy leather satchels.

Slash pierced some poor fellow who toppled backwards down the hatch and fell at the feet of the screaming women.

"Sorry!" he shouted--then plunged back into the fray.

As instructed, Perry and Birdy and Stinker climbed up--each one on each of the three masts—and started to rip open the sails so they could not hold the wind, and hack at the rope rigging that held everything together.

Captain Bonney was holding an ornate pistol to the head of *el capitán* of *El Gordo*.

Things were going quite well for *los piratas*.

After an initial assault, the officers were more compliant, and the gold was being heaved in sacks down to the longboat where Dr. Stuart was stacking them.

Meanwhile, back on *The Dragon's Breath,* Henry had some new friends to play with: a large brown Norway rat, Tom--Birdy's tabby cat, and a ten-foot blue boa constrictor—which had snuck aboard with the bananas taken on in Jamaica.

Henry was watching the cat--who was watching the rat--and stalking it in a circle.

At that precise moment, there was a thud on deck, and Henry—to his horror—saw an unfamiliar pirate staring at him with a look of surprise.

Soon another, and another swept over the gunwales and stood confronting Henry.

"Who might *you* be?" said the first, with a growl.

"Ah, Henry Gerrit Schuyler," said Henry—giving his full name--like he was in gym class or something.

"Who be yer captain, then?" said another.

"Captain William Bonney. But he's not here. Can I take a message?" said Henry.

"We've come with *our* captain—William Kidd—and we would thank you to leave this Spanish ship in our safekeeping, laddie."

"Captain Kidd? The *real* Captain Kidd?" exclaimed Henry. "The famous pirate?"

The men looked bewildered. "Is there *another Captain Kidd*?" one muttered. "Is there something we don't know?" said the tall one with the red beard.

At that precise moment three things happened.

One, Henry's pistol went off accidentally—hitting one in the knee and causing him to fall down moaning and cursing.

Second, the cat finally cornered the rat and the rat leaped onto the shoulder of the tall bearded one—who screamed at the top of his lungs and dove over the side in sheer terror.

Third, the glittery blue boa slipped off its perch on the mainsail stay and landed on the last pirate—coiling itself around his neck--choking off the man's air supply.

He staggered backward—falling over the side--making a splash as he hit the water.

Henry threw a burlap sack over the wounded one and tied his hands with twine behind his back.

I can't walk but I still can fight! Henry told himself.

"What in Christ's name are *you* doing here?" said Capt. Bonney, as his former shipmate and notorious pirate--Captain Kidd--suddenly appeared beside him.

"Thought ye might like some company!" said William Kidd striking a match on the button of a Spanish officer and using it to light a fragrant Cuban cigar he was biting on.

Bonney realized his mistake. Having come up the port side, he could not have guessed that anyone would have come up the starboard side—but that's just how it happened.

Now the captain of the Spanish galleon was really confused.

"J'you know each awther? *Madre de Dios!*

What is worse than *one* pirate attacking your ship? *Two pirates* attacking your ship! *No te creo! Caramba!*"

"Got anything to drink?" said Kidd.

"No. I just got here. Haven't had time to rummage through the cupboards!" replied Bonney.

"I assume you'll leave enough gold for me and my men, too?" said Kidd.

"Help yourself," said Bonney, waving in the direction of the stairs leading down to the hold.

The fire was getting bad. The sails were catching, the lacquered railings were bubbling and spitting flame.

Perry could not believe his eyes! Two pirate captains--just casually chatting away as the ship burned and smoked, as showers of sparks flew in all directions in the breeze.

But that changed in the blink of an eye as cannon fire raked across the deck and took out the railing on the quarterdeck of *El Gordo.*

The man o' war had arrived with guns blazing and shouts from a hundred voices carried across the water.

"Time to go," said Bonney--looking about for his crewmen.

As he climbed over the rail onto the ladder going down to his longboat, he tipped his hat to Kidd and shouted: "The rest is *yours!*" and with that he and all his men—Perry and the others—were rowing hard back to *The Dragon's Breath* as iron balls weighing at least ten pounds whizzed and splashed around them.

Perry did not look back to see what Kidd's response was—he helped Henry up and took him below so the doctor could bind his ankle.

They exchanged stories and as their ship hoisted sail and pulled away from the fray--they had a moment to share a bite and guzzle a cold beer.

"This is way better than reading about it in a book or watching a movie, Perry," he said.

"Don't get too attached to a pirate's life, Henry.

Remember I told you—we're going to get out of this and go back to 2018 and Brackendale and our real lives! I promise you that!"

Henry was fast asleep and Perry carried him over to the straw where they normally slept and he, too, lay down and was instantly in dreamland, the ship gently rocking...like a giant cradle, to...and fro...and to...and fro...and...

Chapter Fifteen   Captain's Confession

It wasn't revealed until the next day, that Capt. Bonney had actually taken a musket ball to his hip.

Doctor Stuart was attending him when the boys stirred and went to wash before breakfast.

He took them aside and told them that Captain Bonney had insisted that only himself and the two boys attend him in his private quarters.

"Us?" said Henry. "Okay."

So it was just the three of them.

When they went in they could see blood on the sheets and the whiteness of his face. He must have rolled in pain all night long, they realized.

Doctor Stuart said to Perry to pour a double shot of rum and hand it to him.

"Drink this, sir," he said, lifting the glass to him. The captain didn't argue.

"I need to slip you out of your clothes, sir. I need to have a look at your wound."

Bonney looked nervously at the boys. He seemed a little shy to be disrobing in their presence, but then again—he had specifically asked for them to come.

He seemed thinner that he did in uniform, the boys noted--his hair finer without his tricorne hat.

Then something *totally* unexpected happened. Henry would tell this story the rest of his life.

When the clothing had been removed, Captain Bonney lay on the sheet, exposing his bullet wound to the doctor—who gasped!

Henry looked over at the two on the bed.

Then Henry choked and said: "Perry! *He* is a *she*!"

Perry drew near Henry's side—and there on the bed was a lovely pale trembling woman!

"You mustn't tell!" she said. "Promise me on your mother's graves you won't tell!"

"N-no," said Perry and Henry together.

Normally these two would never shut up but on this fine summer morning, they were utterly unable to speak.

So they sat down, partly to not seem like they were staring at a naked lady who happened to be their commanding officer, and partly because their knees would not support their weight at that moment.

"Come boys, I need you here," said the doctor.

"Hold her hip down so she won't flinch when I dig the lead ball out of her flesh."

Perry did so.

"Henry, extend your arm so she has something to grip when the pain becomes excruciating. Give her a cloth to jam between her teeth so she won't bite her tongue."

Henry remembered his First Aid training and just responded naturally to what the doctor asked.

The captain screamed into the cloth and dug her nails into Henry's arm as Doctor Stuart clawed with his metal instrument and extracted the ball.

Perry asked for a compress and the doctor gave him a clean cloth to press against her and stanch the bleeding.

"You'll be alright, sir," said Perry comfortingly.

" I mean 'ma'am'."

It was awkward. The nature of their relationship had irreversibly changed in the space of half an hour.

Perry wondered how to keep from acknowledging her femininity to the other crew.

Start by losing the 'ma'am' and stick with 'sir' he told himself.

The doctor covered her and smeared some ghastly smelling ointment onto the open wound.

"One last bit, Captain," he said.

"Boys. Hold her again. I'm putting sutures in and it is going to hurt."

The captain was brave and did not cry out this time but the muscle in her jaw clenched and protruded from her cheek.

Then—it was over.

"You must rest," the doctor said.

"I want my boys to stay," the Captain said.

Just the way she said 'my boys' made tears come to Perry's eyes.

"Call me if you need me," and the doctor quietly closed the door behind him.

"You don't mind? If I ask you to stay?"

"No, ma'am," said Perry. "It is our honor to serve under you. It is an even greater honor to share your secret life. I know I speak for Henry when I say we would do anything for you."

Henry nodded quietly, sitting near the foot of the bed.

"I want to tell you my story," she began.

"First of all, my name is Virginia—yes, the same as the colony. I, too, was named in honor of the Virgin Queen--Elizabeth I, daughter of Henry VIII.

I am the illegitimate daughter of a Yorkshire monk and a servant girl—some said I was cursed because of this sinful union.

My mother was beautiful and from her I get my red hair and freckled skin."

Virginia pulled the covers up self-consciously and continued her story.

"I was headstrong and always resented that I had been born a girl. Girls are *servants*, girls are swept aside by males who vie for power in this world.

Well, that is not my nature to be disregarded because of my sex. I realized that my destiny was in my own hands, so at an early age I went to sea—disguised as a boy, you understand.

On a British ship I saw the discipline and order that have made our military forces successful. I saw the effect that able leadership can have—even on a band of ruffians, such as you see on pirate ships."

Virginia struggled to sit up and Perry put pillows and towels behind her back and neck and smoothed her covers.

She was still in pain and Perry lifted her left hip so the stitches wouldn't pull.

"I might've been able to continue that life of a commercial seaman. My breasts are small and easily hidden. My manner is bold and I take no insult from any man. I am good with pistol and musket, sword and staff. I do not flinch from a fight and I fight to win!"

Capt. Bonney's voice lifted a little, then fell back to nearly a whisper.

"My darkest moment came when we encountered a Spanish fleet driving west to the Caribbean," she said.

"We were outgunned and outnumbered. The Spanish were ferocious as they boarded our ship. Our captain pleaded we were a commercial vessel and no threat to the King of Spain.

No matter. They stripped us and took our tools and weapons. They raided our galley for food.

One brute saw my bared chest and carried me below and raped me. I was left with wounds that cannot be healed.

That is why I curse them—the Spanish! That is why I turned pirate.

My revenge is to destroy and defeat the Spanish in The New World and take from them their honor and dignity—just as they had taken it from me!"

Just then a knock came at the door and a woman servant announced her bathwater and breakfast were hot and waiting.

She was surprised to see the Captain with his long coppery hair falling on the covers, but did not think any more of it apparently, and made no further comment.

"I'll be ready in ten minutes, Mathilda," the captain said.

Captain Bonney made ready to rise, but before she did she looked at Perry and Henry with soft eyes and gentle gaze, and said:

"I know not what your fate will be, but I will stand by you as you have stood by me."

Then she became wracked with coughs and her servant rushed in.

The boys slipped out quietly and—mounting the stairs in the hatch—saw that the fine weather was gone and a strong easterly wind was tearing into the canvas and blowing wave tops straight into their faces.

    ***

"Is she going to be alright, Perry?" said Henry.

They sheltered behind the longboat that was securely tied to the mainmast and the oaken beams that curved up from below, and comprised the ribs of the hull--that was all that there was between them and the angry seas beneath.

"She's as tough as any man I ever met," replied Perry. "I think it takes more than a musket ball to take our captain out of the game.

Let's get some breakfast before it's all gone!"

Both boys scurried below and presented their bowls to the Frenchman—*le Marquis de Montréal* who had gone to sea to escape his creditors, and found himself a captive cook on a pirate ship.

Nevertheless, his culinary skills were excellent and his temperament agreeable.

Unlike the ladies in the Caf at Brackendale—who yelled if you showed up late at, like, 9:30am--asking for breakfast. And the food the Frenchman cooked was way better!

Topside, Bunt, McGuinty and McComb were having a discussion.

"We need to know where we are in order to know where we're going," said Bunt.

"Agreed," said McComb.

"Where *are* we going?" demanded Mad Dog—hardly in a friendly mood with a gale coming on.

"Well that's just it. I haven't seen the captain for a day and a half, so I have no bloody idea where he is taking us!" Bunt said.

"By my reckoning," put in McComb, "The Greater Antilles are behind us now and the cursed wind is driving us into the Windward Islands where landfalls are few and far between."

"Those are French territory," said Bunt. "I wonder if they'll give us trouble."

"Arghh, we are *pirates*!" said Mad Dog. "We aren't afraid of trouble, matey! We *make* trouble!"

"We need to speak to the captain—the decision is his," said Bunt.

As if he had been called, Capt. Bonney lurched onto the deck from the hatch, leaning on a crutch and favoring his left leg.

"Let's set a course, Mr. McComb!" he shouted confidently.

"Aye, sir. How's the leg?"

"It's not my leg, it's my hip—and it'll be fine.

Now look sharp, shipmates. We are in the teeth of a hurricane, as is common in this season.

Make a course east-southeast for The Windward Islands. I've a notion to visit Martinique again. Lovely port, lovely people."

Then the captain turned and went below, trying to balance the good leg with the bad leg and the crutch and nearly tumbling down the last few steps.

Bunt lashed himself to wheel as he struggled to keep them dead into the wind. If they turned broadside, they'd capsize. It was Bunt's job to see that didn't happen.

"Birdy!! Look alive up there!" Bunt shouted up into the cross trees and Birdy poked his little head out of the crows-nest near the top of the mast.

"Aye, sir. Ready and able, sir!"

The fact was that Birdy was such a small young man—really just a boy—that he had to cling like a monkey to the ropes to stop being carried away in the sixty-knot wind!

"Reef the topsails and tie 'em good!" shouted Bunt who could not be sure he was even heard as the wind began to shriek in that really spooky way when a gale starts to blow.

"Aye, sir," said Birdy.

When he wasn't busy cleaning chamberpots and tossing kitchen garbage over the side, Stinker would often visit Birdy up in his nest.

A sailor's life is a lonely one and every man knew that the company of his companions was sometimes all that kept him from losing his mind outright.

Being nearly the same age, the two scampered about the ropework with seeming delight.

And besides, having two of them made the job happen twice as fast—and Bunt and McGuinty knew it.

At daybreak, the wind had eased and the sails luffed as the pirate ship lowered its hated black flag, and again raised the French *tricolore* as if to say: 'Hey, we're friendly!'

Soon they would put into a French harbor and enjoy some leisure time on *terra firma*.

CHAPTER SIXTEEN   MARTINIQUE

Wanting to escape the hurricane and the memory of the encounter with the infamous Capt. William Kidd, they also wanted to have time to rest and restock their supplies.

An ongoing problem was fresh water--which was difficult to come by. Towns with good wells were literally like an oasis in the desert of a sea that was very nearly a million square miles in area—equal to the size of the Mediterranean!

For lonely sailors, it was always a moment of relief and joy when the emerald color of a Caribbean island came over the horizon.

It was Birdy's special duty to holler from his high perch in the sky "Land ahoy!" and so on this fine early fall morning in 1691, Birdy did exactly that.

The island of Martinique has a port with a harbor that lies at the foot of its volcano Mt. Pelée—'Bald Mountain', named for its bare summit with a plume of smoke rising up to the heavens.

Flags from many nations would stop here and trade metal tools and finished goods for food, water, firewood, and perhaps live pigs. Pork was always on the menu for pirates and sailors alike.

The Royal Navy guaranteed each sailor two pounds of meat per day—by far the most generous rations of any sailor in those days.

Bunt arranged to drop anchor and lower the longboat. As usual, only a skeleton crew would remain onboard for security.

Captain Bonney stood on deck and took a head count, as he always did before and after going ashore.

"Where is Dr. Stuart?" he said.

"Dunno, sir," said Bunt, looking at McGuinty-- Bunt wanted him to take the blame since it was his job to account for every man and woman on *The Dragon's Breath*.

"First Mate McGuinty! Are we missing a crewman?" Capt. Bonney's voice went up a pitch in intensity.

"Ah, p'raps he's below, sir."

Mad Dog signaled to Perry and Henry to go below and search for the physician.

They returned shortly thereafter—shaking their heads.

"Where is the goddamned doctor?!" shouted the captain.

He seldom swore or even raised his voice but the issue of a missing crew member was not to be taken lightly.

A small voice spoke up.

"Captain," said Stinker, "When I was aloft I chanced to see the doctor at the stern on the poop deck—uh, having a poop.

A giant wave struck us aft, and when I looked for him again--he was gone, sir."

"That's just bloody pathetic," stormed Capt. Bonney. "How many times have I told you to tie yourself off when using the loo? Ah? How many?"

"He might not have known the rule, sir," offered Slash. "As he was new on board."

"Now we have no doctor. And I've noticed that some of you are not well, so we'll have to scout out someone in port to treat you.

At least until we can replace Dr. Stuart who—by the way—did a mighty fine job of prying a chunk of lead out of my hip and sewing me up.

I'm all but healed up, and for that—I am grateful. Let us bow our heads in a moment's prayer for the soul of Duncan Stuart."

"Amen," said the captain finally.

"Let's keep an eye on one another shall we? Bunt! Get the boat down and let's get ashore."

One by one the men went hand-over-hand down the rope ladder and dropped carefully onto the thwarts and before long, the boat was pulling for shore.

    ***

People say that strange lights are seen just before an earthquake—sometimes on the mountains, sometimes over the ridges of the hills.

They also say that the sky turns a color of brassy metal not normally seen. The old timers know these things; the youth just scoff.

But the fact remains that there were signs that day-- as if anyone could overlook the fact that the ground was trembling from around ten in the morning, and an ash cloud was forming over the volcano.

Henry knew right away what was going on. He was the geology expert at Brackendale; he knew everything there was to know about quakes and eruptions and crustal movements.

He knew that Martinique was located on the edge of two tectonic plates which were pushing against each other and--from time to time--would release the tension and trigger a major quake.

That happened in the 20th Century in Haiti and Puerto Rico when scientists were fretting about something Science did not even know about in 1691!

In 1691, the calendar had been changed by Pope Gregory in Rome and Shakespeare was writing his famous stories about Italian nobility.*· Science was formally birthed in the next century by Newton, Kepler, Copernicus and other great investigative minds.

So it was only when the rumbling from the volcano became a deafening roar that the poor citizens of Martinique realized that the Day of Doom had arrived!

Bonney and his crew ran full-speed to the shore with whatever they could carry, and shoved the longboat into the surf.

·See: Perry Normal and The (Riddle of) the Time-slips

The ash cloud formed a huge grey canopy over the mountain and the sky over the town began to rain stones that burned everything they touched.

Thatched roofs caught fire, horses panicked and overturned their wagons, children screamed in terror as people fled in all directions.

As the crew made it safely aboard and hauled up sail to make their way out of the harbor, an ear-splitting crack shook the air and orange lava began to spill down the slopes.

But that wasn't the worst thing.

What was worse was the grey hot cloud raced ahead of the lava and burned and choked any human being in its path. A pyroclastic flow!

Traveling at thirty-five miles per hour, nothing escaped. In a matter of minutes, the entire port town was in ruins—its people face down in the streets—scarcely a single soul alive!

The water in the bay began to be sucked out to sea, carrying *The Dragon's Breath* and dozens of other boats with it.

Most boats were left stranded in the mud dozens of yards from shore.

The Dragon's Breath had left at the last possible moment--and had gone out beyond the reef into open water where her sails propelled her farther and farther from the ghastly scene.

Henry told Bunt what was about to happen.

"Head directly out to sea and don't look back! The water will return in a dreadful wave and all caught in the *tsunami* will perish!"

"The what?" asked Bunt.

"The wave, man. The giant wave. Ten times the power of the incoming tide! It will finish off the town and any survivors that remain."

True to his word—and to Quartermaster Bunt's eternal astonishment—a massive wave lifted their ship as if it were a toy and passed under, racing toward the beach--but not stopping, now tearing apart structures and houses, uprooting trees, and quenching the volcanic fires with a mighty hiss of steam.

"God have mercy on them," said the captain. "By His Grace are we spared!"

"Mr. Bunt. Steer a course due north for the Bahamas. I have a debt to collect from someone there."

"Aye, Captain." So Bunt pulled on the spokes of the great wheel until the compass pointed to 'N' and the sails bellied out in the fresh breeze that would carry them far from the horrifying spectacle.

The mountain would spew hot lava and gas for three days more until it, too, was exhausted.

By that time, the pirates were well past the British Virgin Islands and Puerto Rico, and heading straight for Nassau which—like Port Royal—was another favored hangout for pirates.

    ***

Ironically, Perry and Henry had begun their pirate adventure by sailing out of a Florida port and into the mighty Gulf Stream. Now they found themselves once more catching the energy of the great undersea 'river' that carried warm tropical water all the way north to Britain and Norway and even Russia.

This last leg now brought the pirate vessel to Nassau on New Providence Island. This 'free' port would be completely governed as a 'pirate republic' from 1696 to 1718 when Blackbeard and other fearsome pirates would finally be hounded out by the British Navy.

Perry and Henry would learn that The Golden Age of Piracy would make its capital here, and terrorize the entire Atlantic seaboard and the Caribbean for decades to come.

So Capt. Bonney and her crew were among comrades as they dropped anchor and rowed into the shallow warm waters that make The Bahamas popular today—although the pirates are gone and tourists and scuba divers much more common.

In fact, it was here that Perry had a narrow escape from a modern-day pirate after lost gold. ¨

By 1667 there were two opposing camps in Nassau—both represented the 'greatest' pirates in history--both were mentored by two different men who were wildly jealous of the power and influence of each other.

Capt. Henry Jennings was the teacher of Calico Jack, Mary Read and Anne Bonny—who happened to be the cousin of Virginia Bonney—known now as William, captain of her own ship *The Dragon's Breath.*

––––––––––––––––––––

¨ See: <u>Perry Normal & The Legend of Lost Atlantis</u>.

Their arch-rivals were students of Benjamin Hornigold teaching pirates much more feared in the Americas--like the frightful Blackbeard--who would set fire to strands of fabric entwined in his beard before he attacked and murdered his victims.

Normally this feud was carried on under the sunny skies of The Bahamas without major incident, as all pirates live by The Code--and conduct themselves according to basic principles of respect and courtesy to other pirates.

One remarkable feature of this Code was that every pirate on ship shared equally in the booty taken from ships that were raided and robbed.

However, it was because of this very clause in the unwritten pirate's Code that had provoked Capt. Bonney to pay a visit to her old nemesis--Capt. Hornigold.

Although Virginia Bonney was not yet thirty, she had paid her dues with pirates since the age of sixteen, and was forgiving to those who were her friends, and ruthless to those who were not.

Hornigold had a bad name among pirates—that she knew very well.

Unlike Capt. Kidd. An old friend. Funny they should meet--while attacking a Spanish galleon full of gold.

But Hornigold was flat-out greedy. He was brutal and cruel. He beat slaves he was carrying to slave markets. He beat his first and second wives to death—for no good reason other than they displeased him.

He was also a cheat. He liked to gamble and drink—as all pirates, and many gentlemen in the colonies do.

It was Capt. Bonney's belief that he had cheated her out of her share of gold taken from a Dutch ship off the coast of New York shortly after it left Manhattan for Amsterdam.

Bonney was a part of the operation and felt justified in claiming her share—just as the unwritten Code provides.

"You go into town, boys," said the captain to Perry and Henry. "I've a little business to take care of."

They did as they were told, and tagged along after Bunt and Pistoff into town—looking for something to eat and drink—and to price the goods in the market.

Perry needed a belt; Henry needed a shirt and some boxer shorts--if he could find such a thing.

Pirates had no dress code, of course. They wore whatever fit them. The only thing pirates were fussy about in their wardrobe was shoes—or boots, as the case may be.

Bonney made for *The Black Swan*—a very popular tavern not far from the docks and the ship anchorage in Nassau Harbor.

The man she was looking for was next door in an extension of *The Black Swan* that was reserved for special customers and their guests.

It was there that she spied her old commander— hair much greyer and girth much larger.

He must be doing well, she thought to herself.

She loosened the first pistol located in the front of her waistband, and felt for the second in the rear--to be sure it was there if she needed it.

She sat a ways back from the table where he was smoking and playing cards.

She ordered a shot of whisky—a drink very hard to come by in the Caribbean but a favorite of her Scottish comrades at sea.

When the play paused, she said in a low voice: "Capt. Hornigold—a word, please."

The overweight and unpleasant man shifted his bulk sideways to see who was speaking.

"Remember me?" she said evenly—her gaze like an animal prepared to kill.

"God's teeth—it's Will Bonney. 'Billy the Kid' I used to call you. You've grown up I see."

He shifted nervously and began to twitch.

"You owe me, Hornigold. I've come to collect what I'm owed."

Suddenly, the tables round the room emptied and a hollow silence descended on the pair sitting facing each other.

Hornigold was used to bluffing his way out of trouble. That's how he avoided being hanged by the governor just last year.

He noticed the pistol.

He said: "You can't prove I owe you anything. And you'll never leave this town alive if you harm me in any way."

"One-tenth of ten thousand Dutch guilders is one thousand," said Bonney. "That is worth £300 at today's prices.

Tell me Hornigold—you scumbag pile of rat shit— how much gold is your life worth? Hmm?"

The big man was sweating. His hands lay on the napkin, his thumbs twirling around each other.

For a long moment, it seemed that Capt. Bonney was going to have to put a bullet into that big fat body since that was the only choice that Hornigold seemed to be giving her.

But suddenly he waved at a waiter, whispered something in his ear, and said one word to Bonney.

"Wait."

She didn't have to wait long.

After all, an important man's life was hanging by a thread and feet move faster in situations like that.

The waiter handed him a purse that must have been heavy as it landed with a thud on the table, nearly spilling his drink.

Bonney knew this man well.

So when she walked over to collect the purse, her pistol was out and its gaping barrel pointed right at his face.

"See you around!" she said and walked through the bar into the adjoining tavern toward the door.

On the way out, she grabbed some fellow's untouched beer and chugged it before he had time to notice it was gone.

The bright sun shone on the wooden sidewalks as Capt. Bonney made her way back to the restaurant where Bunt, Pistoff, McGuinty and the others were already chowing down on what looked like overstuffed burritos and rice.

"We sail tomorrow, gentlemen," she said with a sly smile. Everyone couldn't help but notice the purse.

Then she joined the others as the barbecued pork arrived on skewers. Town food was always a delight!

CHAPTER SEVENTEEN   THE SQUALL

The captain said that she was planning on telling the crew the truth—that she was a woman--and if any man was uncomfortable with sailing with a woman skipper, he was welcome to leave and seek his fortune elsewhere.

"I think that would impress the men, Capt. Bonney," Perry said. "You have been as good a captain as any man at sea, and I think they realize that."

"If anything, it might increase their loyalty—you know, have the opposite effect," said Henry.

"I've been thinking too about giving up the life of a buccaneer—of going straight and buying a piece of land in America and farming it," she admitted.

"It's not to late to find a good man and start a family; I think I'll live longer and be happier," she said.

Perry spoke. "That's what Sir Henry Morgan did, that's what Sir William Phips did. They became not only honest citizens but attained some degree of respect and authority—Morgan in Jamaica, Phips in Massachusetts."

The captain looked sideways at them.

"You know, for a young man you sure know a lot of things. How on earth do you know that Capt. Morgan—that king of pirates—will receive a knighthood and live out his days as a plantation owner? Are you letting your imagination get the best of you?"

She sat down on a barrel and her knees touched Perry's, like they were old friends, like she was one of The Malt Shop Gang.

"We have something to tell you, Captain, something we could never tell you before."

Perry looked at Henry and Henry nodded.

"Where we come from is not a *place*, as such—it's a *time*. Our true home is in the Future and we are time-travelers from the Future.

We left our port—not too far from here as the crow flies actually—and disappeared at sea, swallowed by a mysterious force that propelled us back 327 years to the exact spot you found us adrift in our strange little craft."

"That funny boat with no sails?" she said.

"That funny boat that was never meant to sail, as it had engines and a propeller to power it through the water," Perry continued.

"I'm sorry that I burned it. That must have upset you," she said.

"It certainly gave us the feeling that we were not going home anytime soon," he admitted.

"So what kind of place is it—the Future?"

"Things change a lot. Empires rise and fall, new nations are born, cities become dense centers of population with millions living and working together."

Then Henry spoke.

"Science becomes almost like a new religion as fundamental laws of the Universe are discovered and explored. New ideas challenge Man's deepest beliefs. Fantastic new technologies you would not imagine become commonplace as the globe is mapped and conquered by modern invention.

We have giant metal craft we call 'aircraft' than can fly aloft to Europe in a few hours! We have metal craft that can sail under the sea for months—and visit any land they like!"

Captain Bonney was staring in amazement, eyes wide, hardly knowing what to ask, what to say.

"I can tell you that your idea to give up your seafaring ways is a sensible one and that Virginia and Carolina and Pennsylvania are fertile lands that will be filled with good people—settlers and pioneers—and they will prosper there."

"I know I shouldn't ask but—is there no way for you to travel *back* to your land, *reverse* the curse that took you far from your homes?" she said.

"My life has been a strange one," said Perry.

"This isn't the first time I have time-traveled. I have no real way to explain how or why it happens. The difference now is that poor Henry was dragged along with me, so we are castaways on the shore of Eternity!"

"And what happened to your other captain—Dean? Was that his name?

"He was content to stay in the world of the Past and that is why he remained in Port Royal—as happy as I have ever seen him.

And why not? We have no prospects of returning to the Year 2018 that I can see," said Perry.

"So what can I do for you?" Virginia said.

"No more than you have," said Perry. "You gave us something to do and accepted two shipwrecked boys into your family of pirates—which by the way, relates to a fantasy most modern boys have!"

Perry was blushing.

"What fantasy?" she said.

"To sail the Spanish Main, seeking gold, pretending we were pirates—beyond the law, free spirits, masters of our own destiny!"

Virginia laughed and laughed. "Oh, come on! You're not serious!"

"Really!" Henry said. "And they write books and make movies about pirates, too!"

"Movies?"

"Moving pictures through a technology called photography --which allows us to see people in action on a flat screen—just as if it were happening in real life--although you are sitting in a seat in a theatre munching on popcorn!"

"Oh, Henry, I think that would be fun!" she said.

Henry sighed. "I would give all the gold on *El Gordo* if I could take you back to my hometown and go to the movies with you."

She said, "I am homesick for a stable life with a husband and a farm in this new country you have called The United States."

She stood up and brushed her waistcoat.

"How about we do it this way? I will plot a course for the Carolina coast and we will go on a tour up as far as we can go—perhaps to Boston even.

Then we might feel better, more inspired to believe that there is a future for all of us. What do you say, boys?"

"I say Great!" said Perry.

"Totally!" said Henry.

"Good. Then it's decided. I will instruct our navigator Mr. McComb to chart a course—for America!"

Perry could not help it, so he just threw his arms around Capt. Virginia Bonney and squeezed.

Henry came from the other side, so anyone watching would have had the amusing spectacle of two scruffy young pirates clinging to their captain!

Capt. Bonney put off the announcement about her gender for the time being.

Time to set sail for the Carolinas!

The wind was fresh and blowing behind, so they would have a tailwind that allowed them to run with full sail.

Captain Bonney took his/her customary place on the poop deck—the quarterdeck—and took out his/her spyglass to see what the contours of the coast of Florida and Georgia might be.

***

Curiously, on his second voyage to The New World from Spain, Cristobal Colon—known now as Columbus—passed through a portion of The Bermuda Triangle and noted in his log the appearance of mysterious lights and unusual colors in the sky.

Although she did not know it, Captain Virginia Bonney had been inside this zone since she had left Nassau. It was a fact not lost on Perry and Henry.

"What if...?"

"Say nothing, Henry. Don't get your hopes up! Who's to say we might not time-travel even further *back* and find ourselves walking with dinosaurs?"

"That would be interesting! I'm cool with dinosaurs!

"Sure, as long as they are in *National Geographic*!" Perry said.

The weather was deteriorating rapidly.

Without NOAA or a media weather report, it was impossible to tell what the day's forecast was going to be.

But the waves were crashing on deck with increasing ferocity, and the sheets and stays holding the sails in place were howling like demons.

Quartermaster Bunt had lashed himself to the wheel once more and was slipping and sliding on the quarterdeck as the ship listed from port to starboard and back to port again—at least 15° each time by Perry's estimate.

Every person at sea knows one ineluctable truth— the sea is far more powerful than any ship made by Man.

The Dragon's Breath was a sturdy vessel but she was taking a pounding!

Not only was it nigh on impossible for Bunt to control the rudder and steer her through the deep troughs of the boiling sea, but the compass in the binnacle was spinning out of control—useless as a guide to direction!

All at once, a peculiar pastel mist enveloped the boat--right up to the crows-nest where Birdy was also hanging on for dear life.

Perry took Henry's hand. "This is it. We make it or we die, Henry."

"It's been nice knowing you, Perry. I can't think of anyone I'd rather die with than you, my friend."

There was nothing else to say.

The mist swallowed the ship and the boys felt the maelstrom whirling around them, spinning—around and around.

All of a sudden they felt the warm water of the Gulf Stream, smelled and tasted its own unique saltiness.

The shore was still a long way off although they could see the white beach and the green belt of palms behind it.

The storm? The ship? Vanished!

"Swim, Henry, swim!"

The two boys—fully-clothed and filthy dirty—slowly fought their way through the strong current and would soon discover that they were still on course for Florida after all!

Only--three hundred and twenty-six years in the future!

CHAPTER EIGHTEEN   GUARDIANS OF THE COAST

As long as there have been sailors, there have been ports where men and ships can rest for a time, and make repairs, and gather the courage to continue their voyages in uncharted waters with uncertain outcomes.

The map of our world has been filled in by adventurers and explorers—all seeking to know what lies beyond the horizon!

Today, the coastline of most nations is protected and defended; in the United States, that is the job of The Coast Guard. Their motto *Semper Paratus* means 'Always Ready'.

Founded in 1790, The United States Coast Guard is a branch of the armed services under Homeland Security and actually has the world's 12th largest naval force.

It undertakes missions in wartime but it's best known for its Search & Rescue operations along an unbelievable 95,471 miles of shoreline--from Alaska to New England!

Close to 90,000 personnel—at least half on active duty—comprise this remarkable organization whose job is mainly to enforce maritime law, and ensure the safety of vessels and persons at sea.

The phrase 'at sea' includes everything on or over coastal waters: commercial ships, pleasure boats, aircraft.

As it happened, 7th District Air Station in Miami was on a mission today to locate a missing aircraft flying from Ft. Lauderdale to Freeport—in the Bahamas.

This was almost the identical route that Captain Dean and his *Mary Celeste* had followed some weeks back. Only she was never found--since they never put out a distress call to the Coast Guard to begin with!

They didn't have time! Or to put it another way— Time had *them*, swallowed them--leaving no trace.

As it turned out, the Coast Guard could find no sign of the missing aircraft that had been briefly crossing The Bermuda Triangle.

But in their careful search of the waters off the Florida coast, one clever ensign noticed what appeared to be two persons struggling in the surf offshore, and the pilot of the powerful Sikorsky S-70 banked his helicopter at a steep angle to get a better look.

When they pulled the two boys up on the hoist, they realized that two lives--that would surely have been lost--had been saved.

Coast Guard recruits are drilled in not only physical fitness or weapons and tactical skills, but also in three core values: Honor, Respect, & Devotion to Duty. These are the kind of men and women that comprise our Coast Guard.

And every day they save dozens of lives. Lives like those of Perry Normal and Henry Schuyler.

They radioed ahead and the news was relayed to two anxious families in Upstate New York who were waiting to hear from their sons--who had been reported missing.

By the time the helicopter had landed in Lauderdale, the parents were on a flight to Florida.

***

They were checked into a local hospital for observation, and found to be in good health and without injury.

The doctors and the Coast Guard officer asked how they came to be out there 'paddling around in the drink'--as the officer put it.

They decided the truth was the best option.

"We were doing some fishing," started Henry. "Then some rough weather came up and swamped us."

"Yeah," said Perry. "Our skipper Thom Dean--out of Ft. Lauderdale—he went down with the boat."

Perry gave as many details as he could remember—like the name of the vessel, its registration number and owner, their course at sea.

The Coast Guard would record all this and notify the appropriate authorities that Capt. Dean and his boat would not be returning to port.

'Lost at sea' was how they actually entered the information in the last box of a very long form.

By the time all the interviews and paperwork was done, Lisa Normal and Sherry Schuyler were holding their sons close, murmuring words of relief and comfort, and profusely thanking the Coast Guard officer for saving their children.

"It's what we do," she said modestly.

Just before she joined the helicopter crew for the return flight to Miami, she turned and said to the boys:

"Next time, wear your lifejackets please."

And with a broad smile, she climbed aboard the Sikorsky as it twirled and shot into the sky.

"There will be *no next time!*" said Sherry. "I'm not letting you anywhere near a boat, Henry," she said firmly.

The families stayed overnight in this popular seaside community at the same hotel as before· and that gave them all time to just unwind and catch up.

  ***

It came as no surprise to anyone that almost immediately after they got back to Brackendale, they jumped on their bikes and raced at breakneck speed to the center of their middle-school world—The Malt Shop!

And to their utter delight, all their friends—the Gang—were there, just like always, eating their faces off and laughing and telling stories and planning plans for what to do on the weekend, or on Hallowe'en.

"Oh...my...gawd!" said Charmaine so loud everyone could hear her and turn their heads.

· in <u>Mystery of Lost Atlantis</u>

"Hey guys!" said Perry casually—like they had not been gone at all, like they had not been on the most intense adventure ever—being pirates!

"Hey! What's up Normal?" said Randy the Gorilla who actually came over and shook Perry and Henry's hand.

"We were chillin' in Florida for a bit," said Perry.

"Then we took a cheap flight down to Jamaica to check out the old pirate capital of Port Royal. It was cool! Lots of taverns and open air markets and guys who dressed and acted like real pirates," he went on.

Henry was holding his breath. Perry was going somewhere with this, but where?

"We were drinking beer and eating spicy food with guys who had just come off sailing ships all moored out in the harbor."

Then Perry dropped a bomb that Henry had totally forgotten.

"Look! Before my cell died I got some pictures."

Everyone jammed into the one booth and gawked at Perry's phone.

"This is Capt. Bonney, and this is a dude named Slash who always carries a nasty blade in his belt, and this is..."

There were ten images only.

But that was enough to convince the Gang that they had had a marvelous time hanging out with 'pirates' in Jamaica.

"This was Port Royal?" asked Robert. "The *real* Port Royal?"

"Yeah, of course. It's on Kingston Bay. A real tourist destination, as you can imagine," said Perry smoothly.

Robert whispered something to Max and to Randy and then turned back to Perry.

"I hate to break the news, Perry, but Port Royal, Jamaica—the pirate stronghold—was destroyed in the Spring of 1692 by a massive earthquake, and what was left standing was trashed by the *tsunami* that followed."

You could have heard a pin drop! *Was Robert calling Perry a liar??*

Perry felt numb. But he had to say something—anything--in response to Robert.

"Yeah, I know all that," he said casually, "But the Tourist Board of Jamaica has built it up again to be just like it was in…1692."

Now he was making it up as he was going along! There was no other choice.

"How else would I get these cool images of the old town and pirates--if it didn't exist?" said Perry.

The others looked at him strangely for a moment.

They knew very well that Mr. Perry Normal was inclined to do some very unusual things and have some very unusual experiences.

But…he had his story, and the photos to prove it, and it was highly unlikely—ridiculous really-- that Perry and Henry had just somehow time-travelled back to the Golden Age of Pirates and met real pirates in Jamaica, and just happened to take a selfie with them.

Or *was* it?

The End.

All the Perry Normal Adventures are available on Amazon.com in paperback or Kindle Editions. Check it out!

Also check out the Author Page for Mason Stone on Amazon.

Books can also be ordered directly from the publisher: Red Pine Publishing by sending an e-mail inquiry to:

myredpine@gmail.com

Subject: I want Perry!